THE LAST DEVADASI

Barbara L. Baer

Published by Open Books

Interior design by Siva Ram Maganti

Cover image "Shruthi" © by C Fotografia

Learn more about the artist at www.flickr.com/photos/ wide-eyed-wanderer/

ISBN-13: 978-1948598088

For the two Michaels with love

Dasis or Deva-dasis (handmaidens of the gods) are dancing girls attached to the Tamil temples, who subsist by dancing and music and the practice of 'the oldest profession in the world.'

–E. Thurston and K. Rangachari,
Castes and Tribes of southern India, 1909

"We have a song," Rani said, "Everyone sleeps with us, but not one marries us. Many embrace us, but no one protects."

–Quoted from "Serving the Goddess," William Dalrymple,
The New Yorker, August 4, 2008

"Balasaraswati is a dancer whose name is synonymous with Bharatanatyam."

–Satyajit Ray in his 1976 documentary film, *Bala*

Before

The crying baby girl arrived without a name, wrapped in a white swaddling cloth, on the worst night of the monsoon, the eve of the Nativity, December 1957. A young novice, Thérèse Bellefeuille, heard a cry outside and forced open the door against the wind and rain. She gasped when she looked into the woven basket tucked against the chapel door. Typhoon force winds were sending unmoored small craft up and over the Pondicherry esplanade, and flooding had almost reached the Couvent de l'Espérance Perpetuel, but the basket, sheltered by the overhanging roof, miraculously had stayed dry. Thérèse crossed herself, knelt and picked up the baby who stopped crying in her arms.

La Mère Agnès, abbess of the convent, a former nurse who had arrived in the French enclave as a young novice herself, took the baby in her arms. She guessed the girl to be between four to five months. She was small and dark skinned, vigorous, with bright black eyes and a smile at the corners of her lips. The baby seemed unafraid of the new faces and voices hovering around her. She clutched in her hand a frayed piece of rough woven cloth, suggesting to La Mère that the mother was an Indian woman of few means, perhaps a Christian as the poorest often were.

Christmas Night, with the storm still howling over the Indian Ocean, red-haired Thérèse held the bottle of warm milk to the baby's small open mouth as the *Soeurs* ended their prayers in the chapel. One by one, the women came to gaze reverently at the baby named

Celestine Marie and given an August birth date because every child had to have a date on her certificate. The next morning, Le Père Albert baptized Celestine Marie at the Sacred Heart of Jesus Cathedral to wash away her original sin.

The convent itself was an unremarkable assembly of squat white-washed buildings behind thick walls a half mile from the esplanade and the sea. Within the compound, the smaller building served for the *Soeurs* simple rooms, the larger the orphan girls' dormitory. A school room, kitchen, infirmary, and a well-proportioned small chapel stood apart, shaded during the hot months from the equatorial sun by a small grove of mangoes. In a garden plot, the *Soeurs* grew vegetables for their own table and for the girls, but the religious were aging except for Thérèse, who had arrived almost as mysteriously as had the baby Celestine Marie. No questions had been asked then because the sturdy girl with a Marseille accent, copper curls and a freckled retrousée nose, seemed traumatized, barely able to speak. She asked for shelter and was given it.

Thérèse fit into the *Soeurs* regular life of prayer, teaching and chores. She worked long hours in the gardens, and when Celestine Marie arrived, took over care of the infant as if she'd been her own long-lost child. As Celestine Marie grew, she was never far from Thérèse's side. They sang French hymns and lullabies, and as they gardened, merry songs of sailors. That Thérèse had lived a life she did not speak about was a secret the Abbess did not question. La Mère knew of Thérèse's solitary walks along the esplanade in the early morning after matins, and that she'd been seen staring out to sea. The wise older women would wait for Thérèse to speak of her past, if she wished to.

On Christmas Eve when Celestine Marie was six, she missed midnight Mass at Sacred Heart Cathedral to sit in the small, two-bed infirmary holding cool cloths against Thérèse's burning forehead. The Dengue fever has been particularly deadly that year; four children and two old men in the town had died while the *Soeurs* nursed them. Thérèse muttered strange cries and whispered the name *Pierre* to Celestine Marie.

The day after her fever finally broke and Celestine Marie left her in a deep sleep, Thérèse disappeared. The *Soeurs* called French and Indian authorities, but the young woman could not be found. Celestine Marie sat in the chapel, certain her beloved Thérèse would be waiting if she prayed long to Jesus. She sobbed quietly, holding the lock of Thérèse's copper hair fallen during fever.

Celestine Marie held onto the memory of Thérèse's pale, freckled face every time they recited the Psalms. The lock of red hair remained as bright as ever tucked in her Bible, as bright as the *flambouyant* petals after monsoon. Smoothing the hair between her fingers, the girl rocked back and forth, holding it against her heart, and repeated the words of the child's prayer to Jesus. "Thou art gentle, meek and mild; Thou was once a little child."

Celestine Marie's precociousness in her studies surprised everyone. She learned to read both French and English before most of the girls could parse out simple sentences. Still, La Mère waited until Celestine Marie was ten years old to recount the story of her origins. La Mère, whose pale blue eyes were so opalescent with cataracts that she saw the world as if through a veil, laid out a plate of sugar biscuits.

"*Il y a une fois*. Once upon a time there was a princess born at the very south of India so her skin was darkened by the sun. In time, she married a seafaring man in the French navy and they came to Pondicherry because our little city still belongs to France. You, dear child, were to have been on your way to the Motherland when, on the eve of our Savior's birth, a cyclone of such devastating size loomed on the horizon. Fearing the violent tossing of the ship would harm a babe, your mother came ashore to entrust you to us for a night. Thus you were saved, my child, of the tragedies that occurred that dreadful night. Ships in the harbor were tossed about like toys, while giant waves swallowed up all those near the sea. Your parents were taken to their watery grave, bless their pure souls." La Mère crossed herself and Celestine did the same.

Celestine Marie ate the sugar cookies and tried to visualize a ship flying the French flag in which her mother, an Indian princess, and her father, a captain wearing a white hat and a uniform, disappeared beneath the waves, but her mind fled from imagining such a scene. She had been afraid of the ocean even when Thérèse held her hand and told her there was nothing to fear from the warm gentle wavelets. If other girls played in the water, she kept far up the sand.

La Mère closed her eyes and invited Celestine Marie to kiss her cheek and say good night.

"Now you know, ma petite, from where you came," she said.

But in her own narrow cot, Celestine Marie wasn't sure of anything. She wrestled with the story then and for years to come. She knew she did not look like a princess; her friend Salomé, a girl with honey-gold skin and green eyes, could have been that princess but Celestine Marie, with her dark skin, was not. Earlier, she had overheard La Mère and Soeur Léonie talking about Salomé's mother, a Syrian Christian from Kerala. "How a woman gives up such a fair-skinned girl, only our Lord knows," Léonie had said. To which La Mère replied, "She cannot match our Celestine Marie for intelligence and understanding. For the one we will find a husband but for the other, our Celestine, we will keep her with us and she will be a teacher."

In the convent library, the lives of saints and illustrated homilies were kept on shelves within reach of the younger girls. Books higher up in the paneled reading room contained more worldly stories by French writers. Celestine Marie climbed higher each year until she reached the very top, to the glassed-enclosed shelves where novels about the men and women of Paris could not be taken out without a key.

"In Montmartre and the Bois de Boulogne," she began her nightly recitation to the girls huddled around her, "handsome gentlemen rode in carriages and rescued poor seamstresses and orphans like us. The chosen girls were bathed in cologne and dressed in silk before they were brought to a gentleman's table where they were offered chocolate *éclairs* and *tartes aux pommes*. They could eat as much whipped cream as they wished."

No one ever went hungry in Celestine Marie's stories; no sweets were denied. She had read in an old *Gastronomique* the names of confections and their preparation; the most exciting parts of her stories were not being smothered in kisses but drowning in *éclairs*.

Celestine Marie's quest for sweets led her to various extra tasks. The *Soeurs* called on her to manage their correspondence with British authorities because she could take French dictation and translate to English. She brushed *Soeur* Marthe's hair and rubbed her neck and shoulders for extra slices of bread with honey. Old *Soeur* Jeanne Claire, nearly blind, gave the girl *paisam*, milky rice with almonds and raisins, for reading aloud the descriptions of royal weddings from colored magazines printed years earlier in France. When the old lady, bald and dreamy, was relaxed, Celestine Marie asked *Soeur* Jeanne, "Why do we no longer say prayers for Thérèse? We say them for other *Soeurs* who are gone to heaven." *Soeur* Jeanne Claire replied that Thérèse had left the order and was in France. "She lives in Toulouse, where she came from, with a blessed adopted child, a girl like yourself." Celestine Marie asked why Thérèse would leave India to adopt a child in France when so many here in India waited to be given a home. "I believe there was a man involved," Jeanne Claire said.

2.
Madras, 1975

Kamala Kumari took quick little steps along a parapet that wobbled above a blue tarp printed with white wavelets. Bright camera lights outlined her aquiline nose, full pensive lips, swooping dark brows. A rhinestone-studded blue chiffon scarf loosely covered her hair. The close-up centered on her powdered cleavage, modest enough for the censors, provocative enough to make men in the balcony seats lean forward.

The overhead mikes picked up loud clanking in the background. Distracting noises, traffic and horns from outside the Gemini Studio gate, increased the din. Kamala turned for a full face close-up only to break out laughing.

"Murthy, are there a thousand men in chains below or is monsoon coming early?"

"Sound is too loud, Murthy!" shouted M.K. Prabhan, the director. "But you are not to break from action, Kamala Kumari. You are searching, searching for your sailing ship."

Wavelets appeared to surge each time two *peons* pulled the painted sea-tarp on either side. *Pirates of the Coromandel* was being filmed on limited budget even for a Gemini Studio picture. Though there was little scope for the actress's character development, her brigand-hero, the pirate captain whose ship approached, was played by Ravichander.

Audiences had chosen Ravichander as the rising male star and his films always made money; appearing opposite the beloved action hero could be Kamala's break out from starlet to star.

When Prabhan gave the word, Kamala clasped her ringed fingers above her breasts and opened her glistening lips to sing. She had perfect pitch from classical Karnatic training, but no one would hear her contralto. A playback artist with a higher register would dub in the songs in a recording studio.

"Stop and print!' shouted Prabhan. "Very pleasant, my dear," he said to Kamala.

"Pleasant? Shouldn't there be more emotions? Is there not dread and passion combined here? If only I had lines to speak."

"An image is worth a thousand words." Prabhan walked toward Murthy. "No time to waste. We've got Gopu waiting with his serpent. God willing, there will be light for the scales to show up. Snake scales are *key*."

Director Prabhan was a smallish man with a neat round tummy he was fond of patting. Murthy the young cameraman had not yet been able to grow more than stubble to cover acne scars on greasy skin. His clothes smelled of curry sauces. "His mother's preparations. He is still being coddled like a child," Kamala whispered to Celeste.

"Scales are *key*!" Kamala mimicked. "What about acting and story?"

"Kamala, be quick and change for the serpent scene, that's a good girl. We're talking *Veiled for Love* now. Think Shakespeare's Cleopatra. Tell your dresser girl to hurry with the hair-piece."

"Her name is Celeste and she speaks the French language," said Kamala.

"Very nice Frenchie girl." Murthy wiggled his fingers from behind the camera.

Kamala knew that argument with the director for more screen time was useless. She was grateful to Prabhan for the two roles, at the same time she mocked the way he shot two or more films in alternating scenes that gave his actors little chance to go deeply into their parts. Prabhan prided himself on efficiency and had promised the studio to bring out both films within the year. She would give up all thought of *Pirates of the Coramandel* and prepare herself for *Veiled for Love*.

Veiled for Love, set in an eighteenth-century Nabob's court, starred Shanti as a Mohammedan princess who, years earlier, gave birth to an illegitimate female child she has kept hidden in the harem among dancing girls. Kamala's character, the daughter Narduz, chafes at her seclusion and sneaks out to the river to pursue a love affair with a bargeman. Shanti, an established Tamil cine star, a household name, would have first billing, but Kamala was determined to stretch the range of her character, to give Narduz individuality in this final scene: planning to run away with her lover the bargeman, Narduz learns he has been caught and killed. Thus the tragic ending, pressing a cobra to her breast, Juliet forsaking life for her Romeo.

As she walked toward her trailer to change costumes, Kamala pulled off her wig and shook out her hair. At her dressing table, she powdered her face with one hand and sipped on a small cup of gin with the other. Celeste, her assistant recently hired away from the Connemara Beauty Salon to do her hair on the set, pinned jasmine and paste jewels into her wig. Her young helper spoke the beautiful French language as well as English. Merely hearing the French words gave Kamala a feeling of seeing Paris, her dream city

"More jewels hanging from your bodice? Shall we place them here?" the girl asked.

Kamala laughed. "I'll make do with arm bracelets and diamonds on my wrists. What about the jeweled belt over the sari?"

Celeste held up a studded belt. "I don't think this will suit, Kamala. It will accentuate your small waist but do nothing for your stature."

"You're right, of course. Why am I not taller! What sin did I commit in a previous life that I cannot grow to Shanti's height?" Kamala hated having Shanti look down on her.

"I believe that in France, the most popular singer is Mademoiselle Edith Piaf, a petite woman, less than five feet in height. I have read also that the actress Sarah Bernhardt, who traveled the world performing, was only five feet and quite stout, but she is known to history as a beauty."

"Celeste, you have wisdom beyond your years and know how to lift me from my doubts."

"Be ready, Ladies!" The director's voice came from the other side of the dressing stall. Kamala squeezed drops of belladonna into her eyes to make the pupils more luminous, drew a line under her eyes with fresh kohl, and repainted her lips the brightest shade of carmine.

"Will the kohl not run?" Celeste followed Kamala from the trailer.

"No, it's good after it dries a few minutes. One must not blink until then, that is all. Celeste, you have studied and learned much. Tell me, is it Romeo or Juliet who is taking their own life?"

"They are both committing the mortal sin," Celeste answered.

"Why would they be doing that?"

Before Celeste could explain the plot, Prabhan called again.

When Kamala and Celeste arrived on the set, Prabhan was speaking to Gopu, the snake trainer. The old man had stick-thin legs, a mass of wrinkles and lumps from his bald brown scalp to his gnarled toes. His hooded eyes sunk deeply in bruised-dark sockets resembled his trained snake. At this moment, the serpent's head and forked tongue shot out of the basket. Celeste and Kamala jumped back but the snake, arched head extended to Gopu, appeared to want its hood scratched.

"Gopuji, I see you have your viper." Prahhan kept distance between himself and Gopu.

"Sivaram and I are ready to perform your wishes," the snake trainer said.

"Dear fellow, we sent our people to alert you to changes in plans. We aren't needing your services at this time."

"Sir, Sivaram, that's my cobra here, and I—we—are counting on work today. You see, Sivarum expects his portion of rats and I must also have my evening meal, though naturally I am not a meat eater."

"My friend, if you had King Cobra perhaps it would be possible, but this defanged old fellow no one will believe. Nevertheless, he shall have his rats for supper." Prabhan tapped Murthy's arm and the camera man extended rupee notes. "We will call for you and Sivaram soon."

"I have no telephone, but I will know when you need me again. Thank you, Sir."

"What does he mean he'll *know* when I need him?" Prabhan frowned as he watched the old man disappear into the bushes with his basket.

"Gopu is a fortune teller. Girls and women come to him with love questions. They would miss a day of shooting if Gopu advised the stars were aligned against it." Murthy lit a *bidi* and exhaled a thick cloud of smog brown fumes.

"Do keep that smelly thing out of my face, Murthy. Listen closely, Kamala Kumari, due to circumstances, we are shifting to strangulation by boa constrictor. Come closer with your French mademoiselle. Come sit here beside me for small talk."

"Perhaps he will have you jump off the parapet," Celeste whispered.

"That was *Pirates*," Kamala squeezed Celeste's hand.

"In a few words, my dear, we have dismissed Gopu and his cobra. The snake goddess has infinite forms." Prabhan removed his wire-rimmed glasses and wiped his brow with a soiled towel.

Kamala rolled her large, glistening eyes.

Prabhan polished his glasses. "Instead of swooning quickly, you will struggle more slowly. Being choked by a boa constrictor is no laughing matter. The boa scene I filmed for *Jungle Melody* was outstanding and shot on a dime, as they say in Hollywood. Murthy, take Kamala's young lady in the cart to get that boa, and mind your manners."

"In Indian cinema, we are enterprising fellows and the camera is key," Murthy swaggered.

To Kamala, Prabhan said, "Murthy has taken a liking to the dark-skinned French girl."

"Director, she is too young for men. I feel sorry for Gopu."

"We paid him for the full day."

"Yes, but he has his pride, and so does his snake, I believe," she answered.

"You surely don't mean that snake can feel anything?"

"I do, actually, but nothing will come between me and my boa."

Kamala was relieved that Murthy soon returned with Celeste who seemed untroubled by his attentions. He lay a six-foot-long, speckled rubber snake on the ground. Around them, crewmen giggled.

"People, mood is tragic. Get in position," Prabhan ordered.

"Ready." Murthy called out from behind the camera.

"Quiet everyone. Places. Action."

The set fell silent as Kamala practiced twisting the splotchy sausage into a noose she tightened around her throat. After some moments of struggle, she fell with a sigh upon a pillow, gazed for a long time at the sky above, and sent a final breath to heaven.

"Don't move, not an eyelash," Prabhan gestured Murthy to roll closer. "Let us look at the face of the beautiful Narduz in death."

Kamala's lips softened into a slight smile, her eyes closed, her eyelashes fluttered. From his angle, she knew the camera was capturing a sexually satisfying passage that the censors would approve of; erotic sacrifice being permitted.

Prabhan folded his fingertips over his belly. "That's a print"

"What! I thought we were only rehearsing!" Kamala stood up and dusted off her sari.

"I did not want you to think, only to be spontaneous, a useful trick I learned from reading the American methods of film production."

A boy arrived with a cooler and passed around tall cold bottles of Hyderabad beer.

Prabhan raised his bottle to Kamala. "Not a dry eye will be left in the theater. If I could, I would put you up there on the marquee equal with Shanti but you know how older actresses can be quite sensitive to younger up-and-comers."

"Thank you, Director. Shall I tell you what inspired this scene?" Kamala sat beside him.

"Please do, my dear."

"Why Anna Pavlova, of course, dancing her Dying Swan. I was present recently at a special film showing of her performance " Color rose along Kamala's neck as she remembered that after the film, at home in their bungalow, she and Jules had loved each other passionately to the rhythm of waves pounding the shore. She wasn't yet entirely cured of the man who had betrayed her.

"Pavlova. I've heard the name. Has she been to India lately?" Prabhan asked.

"The Russian ballerina Anna Pavlova visited India before you were born and has passed on. One of the ballets she was most famous for was called *La Bayadère*. You know what it means?"

"You won't catch me in ignorance twice, Kamala. I know that *bayadère* is our Indian *nautch* dancer, the very dancing girl we have been filming," Prabhan answered.

"Yes. Pavlova danced the part of a *nautch* girl who inspires jealousy in a rival who kills her by placing a cobra in a basket. You see how the cobra is part of history."

"How does dancing tale end?" he asked.

"The *nautch* girl goes to heaven where her former handmaids, dressed in pure white, perform a beautiful number called 'Dance of the Shades.' Perhaps we could have such a scene."

"I like the idea. White—the color of widows. Black and white," Murthy said.

"Why should we return to black and white when we can afford Kodak color! You know what I am always saying: public is jury and judge. There are only three basic plots and nowadays, they are all in color. The director who fails to please will have to give up his fine home and go beg in the temple at Tirupati."

"I only meant, Director, that one scene would be filmed in black and white. It could be artistic." Murthy dribbled beer down the front of his *kurta*.

"Let another direct black and white films about poverty in Indian countryside. Go, my children, rest until tomorrow. Congratulations on a day's work well done."

Prabhan stepped into his golf cart and backed up, barely missing a messenger who was running forward with a telegram.

"For Miss Kamala Kumari Devi." The messenger approached with a yellow envelope.

"From Bombay, I knew it! I am requested." Kamala took a dramatic step backward to clear space around her before she opened the telegram. "From Bombay. I must at once send a reply. Celeste, will you gather things and come, please. Goodbye everyone."

When the two had left, Prabhan said to Murthy "That Kamala is full of herself."

Murthy lit another *bidi*. Prabhan blew away the smoke. "Will you get that awful smelly thing away. I feel such a headache before rains. My wife becomes irritable in the heat, but when the first night of rain falls, it is like honeymoon again. Why have you no wife, dear fellow?"

"I'm thinking how that Frenchie girl looks in her frocks."

"Murthy, you saw the cross that girl wore? She is not for you. Mother and Father would kill themselves if you marry a Christian."

———————

In the trailer, Celeste handed Kamala another icy beer from the cooler.

"Thank you, Celeste." Kamala leaned close to the mirror to rub a frown line from her brows. "Can you do anything about this?"

"I will make it vanish. Close your eyes, please." She applied cucumber cream with a circular motion. "You see, it is no more."

"You are a great solace to me, Celeste. Only one week at my side and I cannot do without."

"Will you wear the blue or red sari?" She dabbed Tabu on Kamala's wrists.

"Hari prefers red, the color of Kama and love."

"I will shake out the red and hold it before you."

"This is only for your ears. The telegram was not coming from Bombay. It was from my home village. My grandmother is not well. She is old but will not give in easily to death." Kamala looked at the girl. "Do you worry about your relations?"

"Sometimes I am very sad that I have no one to turn to. My parents have perished."

"I am sorry to hear this. You will tell me more about yourself when the time comes. But now I must hurry to dress before Gopu comes for a visit."

"The old man with the snake?"

At that moment, Gopu rapped on the door. When he entered, Kamala knelt and touched his twisted toes with her fingertips. She gave him a paper cup of gin, which he sipped with a gleam in his eyes before tipping a few drops to the snake's open mouth.

"So the viper likes gin?" Kamala asked.

"Yes, he is partial to it," Gopu answered.

"Gopuji, I am sorry you were deprived work, but at least you come now to tell me what you see in my future." Kamala extended her right palm, which he turned up and down, studying its lines, stroking her tapering fingers. Gopu was not Kamala's personal astrologer, a position long held by Sarla Behn who gave a reading every new moon, but she wished for another interpretation to confirm Salra Behn's recent warning.

"You have experienced a rupture of late. You see, lines are going in two directions, almost as if there had been a battle."

Kamala shivered though the day was hot. She never intended to let Jules go, only to teach him a lesson, but he'd humiliated her by marrying a woman within a month of their parting. That betrayal she would never forgive.

"However, this is not end to story. I see more on foreign soil." Gopu was speaking so softly that Kamala had to lean down to catch every word.

"Foreign soil? How can that be? I've never been outside India. Tell me, do you see anything of a military danger in this foreign land?"

Her hands shook as she poured gin in Gopu's cup and waited to hear his words. Sarla Behn had made a prediction that danger would come from a military man. Was there to be a war?

"I cannot see that clearly." The old man leaned down to the basket and tipped gin into the cobra's mouth. He scratched the snake's hood above darting, metallic eyes. "There is always the shadow until we are free of the wheel of life and death. You will have choices to make. That is all I am able to tell."

"Thank you, Gopiji. Celeste, please bring my purse and we will send Gopu on his way. I feel too weak to move."

"Thank you, Devi." Gopu backed out, carrying his basket. When he had left, Kamala remained in her seat before the mirror.

"Celeste, do Christians require astrologers to know what will happen?"

"Not that I am aware of. But we are superstitious just as you are. I believe in Christ but also there can be other spirits in certain places, the ghosts of those who still love you."

"That is a strange idea. We Hindus believe the soul will soon be in another material form."

———————

Kamala stepped out into a brilliant sunset and saw Raj Terwari approaching. From a distance, the matinee idol looked slender and youthful, but up close his make up cracked over deep lines around his mouth and she knew his figure was laced into a corset.

Tewari loved telling stories but today Kamala would have to hurry; at the same time, she could not appear disrespectful. She owed much to Raj Tewari who had selected her from a dozen girls auditioning for a small speaking role in one of his films. After the audition, Tewari invited Kamala to his home where she expected no less than returning his favor in the bedroom. Tewari was Gemini Studio's major star. Anything he wished, she was ready to give.

He lit candles but instead of approaching her for kisses, he began to talk about his passion, porcelain dolls. He led her into an air-conditioned room where exquisite dolls from all over the world lined shelves or were posed in scenes of their country. The French dolls were having a picnic while the Japanese girls seated around a miniature blossoming cherry tree fanned themselves.

They had spent more than an hour going around the world with these dolls, and then Tewari called his driver to take Kamala home. They had been warm friends ever since.

"How goes it with Prabhan and his efficiency charts? The man never rests, one bad picture after another. But let me tell you my news. My nephew is to be married soon. The girl's father is a Chettiyar from Adyar, the mother was a singer of origins they do not advertise. The parents are paying a significant dowry. It will be a wedding to remember."

"You don't mean the daughter of Pattu Chettiyar of Adyar on Beach Road?"

"The very one. You are acquainted?" he asked.

"We grew up together and are related. Only yesterday she was talking of her daughter Mira's engagement and now I learn he's your nephew. Is it a love match?"

"Most certainly a love marriage. My nephew is smitten by love."

"Pattu has kept much from me. I will berate her for secrets." Kamala looked at her watch.

Tewari gave Kamala's cheek a peck. "Go to your rendezvous with my blessing."

Kamala now walked quickly because Hari Laksman did not like to be kept waiting. She passed under the studio gates onto Gemini Circle where her newest lover's green Buick stood parked in the shade beneath tamarind trees. She opened the door and slipped in the back seat.

Kamala embraced Hari before they spoke. She arched her back, lifted her face, and kissed him so deeply that Indian censors would have snipped the shot right out of the film.

3.

The white envelope addressed to Celestine Marie, Couvent d l'Espérance, Pondicherry, had had no sender's name above the gold-embossed "Hotel Connemara" on the upper left. Salomé, thought Celestine Marie, and immediately felt guilty for turning her back on girls in the kitchen so she could read the letter without being seen.

Salomé, beautiful Salomé, had disappeared from the convent a month earlier and caused everyone such worry. She had been missing at dinner but real concern didn't begin until the next morning when her bed was found empty and her satchel missing with her few belongings. Because the departure had seemed planned, the *Soeurs* deduced that Salomé had taken herself off, but still they called the constabulary because anything could happen to a tall, fair girl, "who does not have the sense to protect herself," La Mère had told the Pondicherry sergeant of police.

"Is there a likeness of the missing girl?" he had inquired.

Soeur Marthe produced a group photograph and pointed to the tallest girl.

"She is quite a pretty lady," the sergeant said.

"Celestine Marie, tell the officer that the photograph does not show that Salomé eyes are green, and she is fair skinned, though God made us all equal." The Abbess pursed her lips. She would not add that when Salomé walked along the esplanade with other girls dressed in their white blouses and long navy pleated skirts, her clothing seemed to fit her tall womanly figure more tightly than it had when the group had started out from the convent.

Because the *Soeurs* trusted Celestine Marie, she had felt twice as guilty for concealing the letter in which her friend revealed her whereabouts. "Such a grand hotel for Sahibs and Memsahibs. I'm saving tips to send you a bus ticket to join me in the city where there are as many sweet shops as you could wish."

When the bus ticket arrived, Celestine Marie had packed her few belongings, her Sunday frock and her prayer book, and with only a candle to see by, confessed in the chapel before the Holy Mother that she was going to join Salomé in Madras. Then she wrote a note.

"Forgive me, but I must go to our dear Salomé to keep her safe. I shall write every week, and when I have found employment and received pay to buy my own bus ticket, I shall come to visit and tell you everything. Your loving daughter, Celestine Marie."

———

Celestine Marie, her satchel over her shoulder, felt stunned by traffic coming at her in the blazing sun on Mount Road. Buses belched black smoke, cars honked continuously at rickshaws and she dodged a large cow that climbed onto the sidewalk. Any space in the traffic got quickly filled by beggars running with their hands out to stop the cars. Finally through the hot shimmery air, she saw the high white wall of the Connemara Hotel that shone as tall as a castle.

She knew the young man in uniform was looking at her dusty feet in sandals. "I come from Pondicherry. Salomé Thomas is my cousin. She is working as a maid," Celestine Marie said.

"That one!" he grinned. "She's known to all because she has been promoted above other girls. You'll find her in the salon."

She saw her friend seated at a table facing a Memsahib who had her hair in large cylinders around her head. Salomé was dressed like other girls in a pink uniform. Beneath the table where she was working, Celestine Marie saw she wore white ankle socks in black patent leather shoes called Mary Janes, shoes Salomé had yearned for.

The large light room smelled of sweet shampoos and soaps. When

Salomé saw Celestine Marie, she tilted her head toward a door at the side of the salon. Celestine Marie walked past a row of Memsahibs and two Indian women in saris who had their heads hidden in bee-hive shaped metal machines that made loud whirring noises.

Salomé came into the side room where they cried a little.

"You look so pretty now and I see this is a fine place but I promised to bring you back with me very soon," Celestine Marie said.

"You go, I shall never return," Salomé answered. "They will only punish me."

"But they have always been so good to us. What would we orphans have done without them loving us like our mothers?"

"I have not forgotten my true mother. You will be so busy you will not miss those old women telling us what we cannot do. Forget that life and be happy here as I am. Quick, I will show you how grand it is here and then I must return to work."

"What is it you do in the salon?"

Salomé described the preparations for ladies getting manicures, though she was not yet trained to do the nails herself, only to prepare the hands in warm water.

"I have been washing hair of Memsahibs. The hair is so different, so much finer texture than ours, especially the blond ones. The hotel has its own confection bakery. A young fellow there says I am as sweet as the tea cakes he makes."

In the Connemara's immense white kitchen, Salomé got the baker to give them small square cakes with pink and blue frosting intended for the afternoon tea.

"We will go have our supper at the YWCA where you only pay a rupee."

That night, Celestine Marie took up the smallest space in the single bed she was sharing with Salomé because her own room would not be ready until the next night. She watched as Salomé slept with a smile on her face. Perhaps it was easier for her friend to put behind her all eighteen years of their past but Celestine Marie could not. She had to keep herself from crying; La Mère and all the *Soeurs* she loved and had betrayed by sneaking away would be weeping and praying for her.

The next day, Celestine Marie opened the door to her own room, as plain as the *Souer's* bedrooms in the *Couvent* and as sparely furnished with a metal-frame bed, sheets, grey blanket, a cross over the headboard. In front of a small window with bars on it, there was a chair and small table just large enough to place a piece of stationery from the Connemara Hotel to write: She brought out her bible and placed it above the paper.

"Dear Mothers, I have found our lost girl well and safe. We both miss you and are saying prayers morning and night. We stay in a Christian place. We send our love."

———————

When they arrived at the hotel in the morning, Salomé said she would make the introductions. "Mr. Charles is a particular person you must treat nicely as I do. He is in command of all the girls and everything here, from the maids to the salon attendants. I shall call you by your English name because it is easier to say."

"So you'll call me Mary?"

"Mary, that's such a common name. I think Celeste sounds pretty."

"But that's not my name. I won't recognize myself," Celestine Marie answered.

"You don't like Celeste?"

"I do like Celeste, but it will still be difficult to adjust to."

"Only at first. From now on, you are Celeste."

They approached a door at the end of a hall and Salomé knocked.

"Come in."

"Good morning, Sir. I hope you are very well."

"Yes, Miss, I am well."

Celestine Marie saw that Salomé had her head a little tilted on her shoulder so her thick braid twitched across her chest. She was looking up at the man from under her long lashes.

"Celeste is my cousin from Pondicherry, Sir. She speaks excellent English and everyone praises her French. She is a hard worker and always honest. You see she is ready to work now."

Mr. Charles hardly took his eyes from Salomé's twitching braid. "We will give you a try, but if I find you are lazy or leave the least dust in a room, you will not stay."

"No, I shall not leave dust, Sir," she said.

"Miss Salomé, you please stay a moment. Celeste, you can go."

"I am sorry, Sir, but customer is waiting. Thank you, Sir."

Salomé pulled them both out of the office.

"Why did you refuse to speak with him?"

"Because I do not like being alone with that old man. Did you see the way he looks at me? Come, let's find your uniform to wear before he changes his mind."

The first weeks Celeste cleaned rooms for twelve, sometimes fourteen hours a day, but even when she was dropping with fatigue at night, Salomé dragged her to the training class in the beauty salon. "Because this is where we will rise. Here are opportunities."

When Celeste got her first paycheck, she asked Salomé to take her to a book store.

"Don't you want a new pretty frock?"

"No, I want a book to read."

Inside Higginbotham & Company, she stood dazed before the shelves.

"Dorothy Sayers! Georgette Heyer! Such lovely sad stories. All the girls read them because they're the most popular writers. If you buy, then you can lend to me," Salomé said.

"I didn't know there could be so many books in one place. It is so much more than even the library in Pondicherry. Look, here are titles by Indian writers." She stepped close and began to read names she had never heard. Salomé pulled her arm.

"Don't waste money on an Indian. Only foreign ones are good."

The sales clerk, a young man wearing glasses and a homespun tunic, approached.

"R.K. Narayan is our most famous Madras writer, Miss. You might begin with *Swami and Friends,* if you don't mind my being so bold to imagine you have not been in Madras for long."

"What cheek," Salomé whispered.

"Yes, I've only just arrived. I love books but you have so many that I am feeling as if I am in a palace or fairy tale. Books are my favorite pleasure. I cannot make up my mind to choose."

"Our store, Miss, is oldest in the country, more than 125 years ago it was open here. Prince of Wales himself made Higginbothams the official bookseller for his Highness."

"Is that true! How long ago that was and how many books in that time being written and read!" She continued to gaze in wonder around her and then looked back at the kind young seller wearing glasses. Salomé cleared her throat and kept switching the sides of her braid that the clerk seemed to ignore. "This is so boring. Let us go," she whispered.

"I believe you will enjoy Mr. Narayan. I myself have read *Swami* many times. The boys in the story are like brothers to me. The books are not costly editions," the young man said.

"You are wasting your money," Salomé sniffed.

"But this book costs less than the foreign ones because it is made in India," the young man answered.

At the register, the clerk introduced himself as Rangan and gave Celeste a notebook with a blue cover. "No charge, Miss. There is one title of Sri Narayan's you may wish one day called *My Dateless Diary.* For now, this is *your* dateless diary in which you may keep a record of all you see and observe in the city, as if you were to be a writer yourself."

"How can you know I am wishing to be a writer, Mr. Rangan?"

"From the eyes, Miss. You have inquisitive eyes, intelligent eyes."

Celeste felt herself seen, but not in the way she observed that Mr. Charles and other men looked at Salomé.

"Come back soon to tell me how you find Mr. Narayan. We will have tea and chat."

As they walked out, Salomé sniffed again in disapproval. "You'll make nothing of yourself if you allow such ordinary fellows to make eyes at you. Why did he not give me a notebook?"

Salomé took them on a bus heading away from the YWCA. They

got off in a part of the city lit by gas lamps that barely illumined the dark streets. The air was sooty with smells of meat cooking on braziers. Women wore strange dark robes that covered their heads.

"This neighborhood is called Thousand Lights. It is where the Mohammedan people live. There is a special sweet store here I have brought you to try, but first, let us have kabobs." Salomé led her to a smoking grill where a man wearing a white cap was turning over sticks with meat on them. They paid two rupees for kabobs dripping with onions and vinegar. In the sweet shop, Salomé ordered *kulfi* ice sweets. A boy, also wearing a white cap, handed them cold pale squares that appeared to be wrapped in silver paper, with tiny silver balls on top.

"What is this? Do I remove the silver?" Celeste held the cold square in her hand.

"No, you eat it all."

She bit into the flat cake, icy almost slippery and tongue-tingling sweet. Pistachios crunched within the cool hardness. She almost swooned from the pleasure of it.

"Tell me how this sweet is called again."

"They call it *kulfi*," Salomé said.

"First the bookstore, then the *kulfi*. You were right, Salomé, life in the city is more interesting. One day, we will have enough money saved to bring a few of the girls here."

"The *Couvent* is enough for them but you and I wanted more," Salomé said.

"I was content with my portion. Now I realize there is more and I wish to share."

"You were not content, You were always dreaming or reading books, I never knew someone to read as you did. But you haven't yet been to see the Madras beach."

"You know that I am not fond of the ocean."

"We will pass by the beautiful houses where one day I will live. We'll go to the end of the line. Just look at the houses."

They waited for a bus to Adyar and sat in the front. Salomé pointed out white mansions lit behind high walls. "I will live here one day, just you see."

"You will have to save a lot of money."

Salomé gave her friend a look as she might give to a child. "From my savings! I will never be able to afford. I will be living here and I will not be cleaning the house."

The bus stopped at a turnaround. "Here is where you wish to go, young ladies. In one hour, I shall return, and after that, no more buses. Don't talk to strangers."

"We can take care of ourselves," Salomé answered, flicking her braid.

Celeste hung back and let Salomé go closer to the incoming waves because she had never trusted the uneasy moving body of water.

Within a week, the girls' schedules were keeping them from seeing much of each other. Salomé refused to get up on Sunday mornings for mass at Saint Thomas Cathedral, even though it was bigger and more beautiful than even the Sacred Heart of Jesus in Pondicherry.

At work it became easier to answer to her name because the girls called her by that name. "Celeste, come look at how these curls turn up!" "Celeste, did you hear me, go get the tray." Within days, she responded but the name didn't yet feel right because she had been Celestine Marie from her earliest memory.

When Mr. Charles authorized her to give shampoos to the hotel staff, Salomé said she was moving up. Next, she was told to give manicures to the maids, waiters, and busboys, and then, the most demanding assignment, straightening the Anglo-Indian girls wiry hair into smooth bobs. They appreciated her because she never burned their scalps with the straightening solution.

One day, the senior manicurist called in ill and Mr. Charles rushed around until he said, "Celeste, go to Sahib, he is particular about his nails."

She approached the table where the dark-eyed gentleman with a lustrous head of black hair sat with his fingers in warm water. "This is

Miss Celeste. We offer her services, Sahib. I believe you'll be pleased."

The Sahib asked where she came from. "Ah, Pondicherry. I drank a glass of French wine in a café there. Such a difference the French make. Do you speak the language then?"

"Yes, I do, Sahib. We were taught in French. Will you tell me about your country?"

Jules talked about the Netherlands. He described how dikes kept the sea from overwhelming the land as it did in Madras during monsoon, and how he'd once had to live in a windmill.

"I would be afraid of so much water," she said.

"The Dutch are a determined people and we love the sea."

After the end of the day, Celeste went to the British Council library to read in the encyclopedia as much as she could about The Netherlands, that small country always threatened by the sea.

When Kamala Kumari arrived at the Connemara for her manicure and hair appointment, a hush fell over the room as the small, beautiful woman stood with her hands on her hips.

"She makes demands, she's not nice, she changes her mind on nail color," one of the girls whispered. "Doesn't tip nicely, either," another said.

"Send me the French girl Sahib Jules speaks of," Kamala ordered as she sat in the chair before the mirror.

"But Madam," Mr. Charles protested, "you have complaints with Kalyani? She is back and you have always liked her."

"No, but I wish the French girl."

Mr. Charles clamped his lips together and signaled to Celeste to step forward.

"I understand that you speak the French language," Kamala said.

"Yes, Madam, I grew up in Pondicherry."

"Would you say a few words to me?"

She blushed, then spoke several sentences. "*Est-ce que vous avez soif?*"

"And what do those words say?"

"Are you thirsty?"

Kamala clapped her hands. "Is that all! The French language sounds so much prettier for the same meaning. If only I could read the French stories in their own language."

"Which stories are they?" She began working on Kamala's softened cuticles in the warm water bowl before her.

"There is one author, his name is Maupassant, that I would have liked to know."

"I like his stories very much also, but the character and plot in the translation must be fine also." Celeste placed a warmer soaking bowl at Kamala's feet.

"You have gentle hands and a sweet manner, girl. What is your name again?"

"I was named Celestine Marie, Madam, after La Sainte Marie the Virgin who ascended to heaven. *Celestial* is the word for the heavenly in French. Here, I have taken a name easier to remember. Celeste."

"Celeste, I like that. Perhaps I've heard of a film star of that name. Please speak more French words and I will try to repeat."

Celeste coached Kamala through words for pastries and they both smiled.

The salon fell silent and eyes turned as Kamala rose, tied her deep blue sari tightly around her waist and handed Celeste a ten rupee note where everyone could see. Salomé made a little gasp as Kamala clicked across the polished floor in her high heels.

––––––––––––

The next time Kamala came for her appointment, she asked for Celeste again. When her hands and feet were both soaking, Kamala asked, "You know the Dutch Sahib?"

"I had the privilege to serve him. He is well-mannered and learned."

"He has good manners. That is one side of the man. You haven't seen the other."

Celeste felt a moment of shock hearing Kamala's words. Salomé had confided that the Sahib was good friends with the cinema actress.

"Friends, you understand?" The tone had puzzled her and now she was trying to make sense of Kamala's remark.

———————

Kalyani, the senior woman Celeste had filled in for, relapsed from Dengue fever. Salomé wanted her clients so Mr. George gave them to her, except for the Dutch Sahib who requested Celeste.

"Miss Celeste, I have a matter to discuss."

"Yes, Sahib. Shall we change the water in the basin?"

"Wait a moment, please. My wife, who has only recently come to India, has been ill these past weeks with the Dengue fever."

"I am sorry to hear that. I hope she will be well soon."

"She is recovering, thank you, but there is a problem that I hope you can help me resolve. My wife is lonely with no one to talk to when I am gone. I am looking for a reliable and lively person to visit her some hours every few days. Perhaps we should wait because I would not want to expose you to the fever."

"I'm not afraid, Sahib. I have had the fever in Pondicherry and it does not return."

"I am glad to hear that. You appear very competent though you are quite young."

"I am eighteen, Sahib."

"My wife is only a bit older. I think you could be friends. If you agree, I shall speak with your employer to arrange your work here so you can come to our home two mornings a week. I will make it worth your time and be grateful for your help."

"Thank you for this honor, Sahib. I shall do my best, and since my appointments only begin at eleven, and I am up early every morning, I can come before my work here."

"I'll fix it with Mr. Charles."

———————

Before Celeste knew whether Mr. Charles would agree to let her make morning visits to the Sahib, Kamala Kumari returned to the salon where she also had a request.

"I will pay you privately to come to the film set and do my hair. I like talking with you, Celeste."

"Mr. Charles is my employer, Miss Kamala, and I do not know if he will agree."

"Mr. Charles looks like someone who will say yes to money."

After Kamala was gone, Mr. Charles took Celeste into his office. He didn't ask her to sit before he began berating her. "You are making me rearrange the schedules. You are causing me trouble, Celeste. I cannot guess why you are chosen by these people."

"I asked nothing of them. They have asked me, Sir."

"I am twice surprised because your friend from Pondicherry has more charm, but then I would not want to lose her to those people. So Miss, for the moment, I agree to the customers' requests. I'm not sure what plotting has gone into this. You are quite a forward minx despite your country ways."

"There is no plotting from me, Sir. I have been surprised as you are."

"I won't be responsible when you are back saying to me they have deceived you."

"I understand. I am sorry to be troubling you, Sir."

"Hotel management does not look favorably on locals being preferred." Mr. Charles said.

With the first 100 rupees she saved in her locked suitcase at the YWCA, Celeste opened an account at Barclay's Bank and deposited the payments that Sahib Jules made. She kept out ten rupees to spend at Higginbothams.

"I believe I told you my name the last time but I don't know yours, Miss," the young clerk with glasses said.

She paused a moment, still not sure about the name she was going by when it was her choice to decide. "I am called Celeste, thank you. I liked Mr. R.K. Narayan very much and would like to read another of his books. Also, if you have stories by Maupassant in English, I shall buy a copy."

Rangan reached to a shelf and brought a small book entitled *Malgudi Days* to the register. "This is my favorite. In these tales, you will meet Indian characters who seem so real it is as if you are meeting them in life. We do have Mr. de Maupassant in English. I like reading his stories very much as well. May I ask, Miss Celeste, how you are liking the city? You have been many months?"

"Almost three. My head is a little turned by all that has happened."

"You are finding friends, I suppose?"

She wondered if she detected a little disappointment in Rangan's question.

"You remember my friend I came here with? I must bring her back."

"She was not so interested in books as I recall, while you and I, we are lovers of books together." He seemed to blush a little.

"To tell the truth, I feel I'm losing my friend. She is not going to Mass which is a sin. She only likes cinema. I am somewhat behind her in life experience."

"You have imagination, Miss. You and I know more than she does about life from reading in books."

Celestine Marie knew that Salomé would consider this man's remark too intimate, too 'cheeky' as she'd say, but he had spoken a truth she'd known for a long time: through reading, she could know the world.

4.

In the shade of Ahmed Jamal's awning, Jules unrolled new lengths of printed handloom fabrics, stroking one deep grey cotton with its unusual water design and weave. He smoothed his hand over another, burnt orange raw silk that made color rise to his cheeks with the memories it brought. The other men raised their eyes from the bolt of orange silk to watch a row of five coolie women drive their bony cattle ahead of them, barely breaking the rhythm of their stride to pick up the wet cow droppings, slap them into pancakes and press them to dry on the crumbling sidewalk.

Jules admired the upright posture of the women who hadn't an ounce of fat on their bodies, and the confident way they'd tied their faded red saris up high between their legs to be able to stride as freely as men while swinging their hips with distinctive womanly motions.

Small Mohammedan boys wearing white skull caps dashed out to tempt the earliest shoppers toward their stalls. "Ma, Ma, wedding saris from Varanasi, nice infant underclothing."

Jules and Ahmed knew it was too early for matrons to buy. Before she made a purchase, a bride's mother would unfurl dozens of saris when the heat in the stalls was so intense that the primary colors of silk from the Kanchi and Bengali weavers glimmered before her eyes, crimsons and golds shimmering in the sun as bright as marriage jewelry itself.

Ahmed offered Jules a green mango sprinkled with red pepper powder. The men ate the dense, smooth, mouth-puckering flesh cupped in their hands, leaning out over the street.

"It is good to have you back," Ahmed said.

"It is good to return to Madras. When I'm away, I know India is where I am at home."

"And even better that you have returned with a bride, though many ladies will be keeping to their rooms in tears at the news." Jamal inclined his head with a friendly nod.

"Not so many. I was judged a confirmed bachelor for too long," Jules replied.

"A man in good health should not be unmarried, it is against nature," Ahmed said. "Prosperity without wife and children makes a man poor in spirit. Why would we spend our lives here on these streets all day haggling for rupees if not for family? Your business is good, I believe. All that was missing was a wife."

Jules bowed his head a moment. "I am no longer in my youth, Ahmed. My bride is young."

"You are a man in the prime. A bride younger than yourself is proper."

"Too many good words and you'll turn my head." Jules didn't mind compliments. He was vain about his appearance and, at forty-three, feared he was losing his looks. His strong heavy thighs were going soft and the wavy black hair that he pomaded and combed to the right side had begun to show grey. Fortunately a new girl at the Connemara he'd become fond of had touched it up with dye. He'd recently shaved off his mustache because he thought it made him look older.

"Sab Jules," as Indians called him, could have sat in his main, downtown office of Madras Silk and Handloom Trading Company writing up orders while his employees did business on the streets of Georgetown where he had his second business, but he valued contact with merchants who spent their days rolling and unrolling lengths of cloth as if they were precious manuscripts, men of the bazaar who knew the quality and designs of fabrics. Moreover, he felt that Georgetown, the oldest part of Madras, a maze of lanes running from Fort St. George down to the wharves, was where he belonged rather than in the more modern office row along Mount Road. In the evening, when Jules stayed after his secretary had left, he wandered toward the port, following the vapors, the paths of sailors and women in search of a haven to assuage their souls' restlessness.

Jules' father, Henryk Van Steen, was Dutch; his mother, Bella Rosanova (nee Mintz), a Polish ballet dancer. In her late teens, Bella was performing with Anna Pavlova's touring company when the great ballerina died suddenly in The Hague, leaving her young dancers stranded and penniless. Henryk, a man-about-town with eyes for pretty young women, offered Bella his protection. When she became pregnant, they married, but love did not survive the marriage.

Jules was clearly a Mama's boy which Henryk resented. Early memories of his mother still came to Jules, her fragrances, attar of roses and musk mixed with her perspiration in the creamy warm depths of her breasts. Of his father, Jules remembered the smell of alcohol and cigars, tempers and sullenness, of furniture being overturned in angry shouting matches while mother and son tried to avoid the heavy hand falling on them.

When his father told them to pack and rushed them out of The Hague ahead of the German invasion, Jules rejoiced: he'd be taking a vacation away from Henryk with Bella to himself. He had time to choose a few precious books of travel adventures and his telescope. Bella at first made a game of their hiding place with a farmer in his barn before Henryk moved them again to a windmill along the North Sea where waves crashed hard against the coast. Of those years, Jules remembered mostly cold and hunger until the day he and Bella stood side by side in the grey misty air, both of them thin and almost delirious, waving rags at the sky to American pilots flying their planes overhead. The taste of a chocolate bar a soldier gave him he remembered to this day.

Jules never completed high school after the war. At fourteen, tall and sturdily built, he lied about his age and shipped out as a deck hand with the Dutch Merchant Marine. As his ship pulled away from the bombed-out shipyards of Rotterdam, he held back tears, imagining his mother reading the letter he'd left for her.

In Jaffna, Ceylon, Jules went to a prostitute for his first experience. On his way back to his ship, the girl's pimp was waiting on the docks and beat him until he lay unable to pull himself up from a puddle of grease. A pair of stevedores, indentured Tamil laborers brought from Madras State in India, carried him to their shack where they cleaned and bandaged his wounds. Ramachandra and his brother lived in the condition of near slavery, but they gave him everything they had. Jules took Ramachandra's sufferings to heart and remained a loyal friend.

For a half dozen years, Jules sailed on freighters that carried goods between Hong Kong, Singapore, Madras, and Calcutta on the Bay of Bengal, through the Suez Canal and back to Europe where his visited his widowed mother. He learned languages and how to keep records of goods and payments for his captains. By the time he was in his mid-twenties, he had left the sea to manage a shop for a Tamil sari merchant who had branches in Madras and Colombo, Ceylon. He took over the trading company in the Georgetown port area of Madras and opened a second office on Mount Road. Over the decades he'd been in trade, he hadn't consciously cultivated a mysterious identity of a European belonging everywhere and nowhere, but he hadn't fit in with British post-colonials. Indian women he'd known before his great passion for Kamala Kumari had in common being in some kind of trouble, and he had risked harm rescuing them.

———

The sun now burned overhead and the coolie girls were returning to the streets to collect the dung cakes they had laid out to dry. Ahmed Jamal and his assistants tallied their accounts before pulling down shop awnings for lunch.

Ahmed seemed surprised that Jules was not planning to return home to his bride for midday meal and nap.

"I recall these moments early in marriage as the sweetest time of the day." Ahmed looked away so that his meaning would not be so obvious.

"I've too much to catch up on," Jules replied.

On the way to a lunch room, Jules stopped to buy the *Madras Mail* of Tuesday, September 27, 1975. Details of another government scandal covered the front page. Inside, photographs showed Tamil students rioting over the language issue, a feverish topic among South Indians who feared exclusion from government employment if Hindi replaced English for government jobs.

In the crowded lunchroom, fans turned slowly overhead, keeping some of the flies hovering airborne above food on tables. Jules turned to the back of the paper where the shipping pages listed arrivals and departure from the port of Madras. He found The *Midnight Tiger* coming in from Singapore, and the *White Sphinx* from Alexandria, both headed for Jaffna, Ceylon. Later in the day, Jules would send a wire alerting Ramachandra's sons to the arrival of the two vessels in Jaffna because he'd agreed to do so, even though the young men's talk of an armed Tamil uprising grieved their father.

The high warbling of film songs drifted in from the street. Small boys called out between tables while two little girls ran from the kitchen carrying stainless steel plates and cups of milky tea that lapped over onto saucers. On the empty table next to him, a customer had left a cinema magazine, *Cine Starlets*. Jules stared at the image of Kamala Kumari on the cover, her skin lightened to a cream color, her lips a glistening pomegranate red almost as if their moisture actually were painted on the cover. Sweat ran down his face and he wiped it dry with a handkerchief. Why did this picture greet him upon his return when the last person he wanted to think of was Kamala Kumari? This question led to the next: who had Kamala favored to be featured on the cover? He turned over the magazine to avert seeing her seductive eyes.

He cooled his steaming curry with *dahl* and *raita* and began to eat. At home, in deference to his bride's delicate stomach, he had his cook prepare bland dishes. Now he indulged, though it would give him heartburn, in some way less painful than his own misgivings and regrets.

After lunch, Jules spent the rest of the afternoon going over bills of lading and export forms. His Anglo-Indian secretary, Gita, an attractive and competent young woman, was pregnant and working half days. Soon, he would have to hire a secretarial replacement and train her.

At last the sun, huge and orange, began sinking over the cupolas of the Madras High Court. He called his Mount Road office for last-minute orders before setting his packet of outgoing mail where Gita would post it in the morning. In two hours, he was taking his new wife to the Madras Club for supper. He relished the shock and envy the snobbish Brits would feel to see a lovely young beauty on his arm, a pleasure that would help get him through the evening among people who didn't conceal their dislike of him.

He padlocked the outer door and descended two flights of wooden stairs onto Choudry Road, then walked along Old Jail House Road. Georgetown seemed to be suspended in flickering lights when Jules reached the port and saw the rusty hulks of the *Midnight Tiger* and the *White Sphinx* that would be sailing on to Jaffna. These were not first-class ships, just refurbished old freighters carrying goods of all kinds from one port to another. On the decks, he could see tall mounds of coconuts stacked in bundles. He knew from experience that in Jaffna the Singhalese customs officials wouldn't search deeply in the piles of coir or fruit for contraband because of tarantulas, even snakes. He also didn't want to know what might be hidden underneath; what trouble the boys in Jaffna were preparing. He pitied their father to whom he sent monthly remittances because his old friend had injured his back and could no longer work on the docks.

Jules walked to V. Muttiyar Street where the used book sellers stayed open until it was almost too dark to read their titles by flickering oil lamps. He scanned the small volumes until one grey booklet caught his attention. On the front cover of *Problems of Public Morality: The Place of Devadasis in Hindu Society*, a dancer held a provocative pose. The curvaceous woman, arms over her head, her sari tied tightly at her waist, looked to be of short stature, full in bosom and hips, an hourglass figure that was the ideal South Indian woman, one of Kamala Kumari's attractions.

On the back cover of the booklet, the author, an old man named Krishnamarcharia, was posed before a draped cloth, one hand on a sacred Brahmin thread that crossed his sunken chest like a white worm.

The book seller, sacred thread across his plump brown chest, made a chapel with his putty-colored hands. "Dancing girls are special interest to you, my friend. I have saved this for you."

Warm sea air whipped Jules' face and dried his perspiration. He felt an itching, uneasy hot sensation down his spine and into his groin as he read the back cover.

Devadasis are wedded to God because they are the sacred dancers who alone perform a most important divine commission in our temples. They dance and sing and serve rice to Siva. They perform another service: to reclaim lost sheep and bring them into the fold of God. Without their special services, ordinary homes like ours would become secret brothels, husbands would not respect their wives, and diseases would spread more virulently than ever without such abolution.

"Abolution! Do you know the word?" Jules asked the bookseller.

"No, Sahib."

"Well, for your information, the esteemed author has made an unconscious neologism that I find fascinating. He combines your Hindu bathing ritual of *ablution* with a Catholic priest's grant of *absolution* for sin, especially of a sexual nature, along with *abolition*, meaning to end something. Do you find this not amusing?"

"Sahib, the book is written by a most learned man with A.B. degree. I respect learning."

"I am sure you do, and I expect this treatise by a self-proclaimed scholar who doesn't get his words quite right will be riddled with superstition, error and repressed lust."

"Sahib, you have liked my books in the past. Why are you insulting learning?" The bookseller pressed his hand to his heart as if personally wounded by Jules' words.

"Because it perpetuates ignorance." Jules looked from the author's photograph to the bookseller and saw two Brahmins who felt privileged by the superiority of their caste, even as it bound them to prohibitions and taboos against anything connected with sex. Even in marriage, the sexual act that resulted in losing semen was a loss of self and had to be washed away, purified. However, these clever, clever men had invented an escape hatch in the system: girls and women born into the *Devadasi* caste, females classified as Untouchable like those pariahs who carried away waste and the dead, were assigned the sacred rituals of serving the deities inside the temple, while outside, in dark warrens and cottages, they were bound to service the lower parts of the upper caste body: these were the *services* the author of the pamphlet meant without spelling it out.

Jules regarded the entire caste system, like the Catholic Church, as one huge pathology. The key insight in his own research would show how the *Devadasi* caste had been created to reward men who feared women.

He threw his head back and sucked in the humid sea air.

The bookseller cleared his throat. "Would Sahib prefer a volume with color pictures?"

"No, I'll take this one." Jules drew twenty rupees from his wallet.

"I am hurt in my heart at pittance you offer." The bookseller reached to take the booklet.

"Twenty-five." Jules turned to walk away.

"Very rare book. Thirty-five, Sahib, money for family."

Jules counted out more bills and *Problems of Public Morality* became his. If he hurried back, he could hail a taxi and be on his way home to his bride with a clean conscience and body. His physician, Dr. Fitzgerald, had minced no words: the next time he contracted an infection, antibiotics might be of little use. He could hear the Irish doctor who never spared blunt words. "For God's sake, man, get a wife and keep the organ clean for her."

Tangy salt washing over wet pilings mixed with cooking smells, frying onions and coconut oil, drifting from rooms above the warehouses. He stared up at the wooden tenements of the narrow alley and began to walk toward the junction of North and South Beach Roads at Mahatmahaji Row where he would find taxis waiting.

Before he reached the safety of this thoroughfare, he saw the girl on the corner.

She was small, dark, with shapely arms, her toe nails painted pink in blue rubber thong sandals. He passed a man with his back to him, relieving himself on a wall. Is the man her pimp? Jules wondered. Another girl, taller and fairer, stepped out from a doorway. "Sahib, stop for a moment," she called.

Their pimp would assume he'd choose a light-skinned girl, but he walked on toward the corner, where the dark girl had positioned herself against the wall, curling her painted toes as if she remembered the feel of country dirt under her feet. Rings of sweat outlined the curve of her nipples. He asked her name.

"Usha. Sahib, you wish to come with me?"

"Usha, the heavenly dancer."

"Sahib, you are handsome as a Hindi film star so you will come with me." She stroked the tip of her oiled braid that lay across her breasts like a pet black snake, reached into a small purse, withdrew a tube of lipstick and applied its shiny red apple color in a single swipe. She flicked her tongue onto her upper lip where she had a faint mustache and beads of perspiration.

A shiny water bug the size of a frog scuttled across the sidewalk at her feet.

"What a dirty bad place this is for you, Sahib. You'll be getting your fine clothes soiled from the street. Please follow to my room."

"Where do you come from, Usha? Where were you born?"

Usha named a village. "It is called Puddavalli, but you will not know it."

"Yes, I do, Usha. Puddavalli was an ancestral *Devadasi* village."

"I know nothing of that, Sahib."

Usha could be a valuable source, he told himself. A few minutes of questioning the girl and then he'd be on his way home to his bride.

"You are wearing a wedding *tali.*" Jules stared at the gold disc centering a strand of black beads around her neck. This *tali* was exactly the kind of disc that priests tied around the necks of *Devadasi* girls at the time of their symbolic marriage to the statue or symbol of a deity.

Usha looked down at her bosom and tucked the *tali* in her blouse. She began walking.

He followed along Mahatmahaji Row, named after Mahatma Gandhi who had led the ban on dedicating girls to temples. How could that good man have known that this street where girls sold themselves would be named after him?

"Where is your husband, Usha?" Excitement began to overwhelm him. His feet, his nose, his throbbing capillaries were seeking relief all the while his mind was telling him that Usha would be nothing more than an opportunity for an informational interview.

"I was married at ten, Sir. The boy died. You are not afraid that widows are bad luck?"

"No, I pity your hardship. You were unlucky."

"Yes, I have no luck."

He could see that Usha was afraid of something. She looked behind her twice before she arrived at a warehouse, opened an outside door and began to climb stairs with him behind her. On the third floor, she pulled open a door. Inside, a bulb encrusted with dead insects dangled in the center and roaches scuttled to dark corners and vanished into the walls.

Usha stood calmly, her sturdy legs apart.

"I'm sorry that I cannot bathe, Sahib. There is no water here."

"You shouldn't worry. I'm here only to talk with you. Please come to sit beside me and answer a few questions. I will pay you well for your time, Usha."

She sat next to him on the narrow bed and stroked his arm.

"Was your mother connected to classical music or dance in any way?"

"Why should she be, Sahib? I like only sweet songs." Usha smiled and began to sing a catchy melody Jules had recently heard on the radio.

"I know many songs from the Beatles. I love Beatles!" Usha pointed to a photograph of four young men leaning together and grinning at the camera.

"I've heard of them but my interest is in your music in India," Jules said.

"Sahib, I can't be long. Brothers are waiting." She stood up and began to untie her sari.

He held her arm. "Be a smart girl and tell me of your marriage, Usha."

She looked worried. "I told you, Sahib. I am a poor widow since childhood."

"But what kind of wedding? Did they secretly dedicate you to Lord Siva?"

"Why would you say that! Please, I cannot take more than my usual time here. Otherwise, brothers will be angry." As she backed toward the bed, she bumped into a nightstand and knocked a pink box onto the floor. Powder spilled everywhere.

"Oh, look what you've made me do. Now surely I will be in trouble, so be quick." She gripped one of his hands. "Sahib, waste no more time." She backed up toward the bed and undid her *choli* blouse, unfastening the hook and eyes on the front, pulling it off so he saw her breasts, dusky and round, with darker, extended nipples that had an enticing brown ring around them.

He wondered if she'd borne a child. He had important questions to ask but his head was swimming as Usha lay back on the bed, naked except for pink cotton panties. She wiggled her hips. Her legs were muscular like a dancer's. The room was so hot, the air dense and stifling with the smell of the sweet spilled powder that he could barely breathe.

Usha pulled him to the bed, rolled over him and sat on his hips. She undid his zipper and pulled down his white trousers and his underwear to expose his member. As she arched her pelvis toward him, he had a view of her dark pubis and within that, her pink private parts that looked like a dessert jelly.

He could no longer get away. She enclosed him with her strong legs. She covered him.

"Be still, stop moving," he groaned. If she held still, he might be able to regain control and withdraw, but she gave him no mercy, climbing higher onto him, securing his member deeply inside her. She tilted her head back and made small panting cries. Her sounds obliterated the last of his resistance and he let himself go into the heat and darkness of a long wave of release.

He caught his breath and cursed himself as he wiped off with a dirty towel. At the door, he paid in large bills.

Usha begged him to make a date for another evening, to become her husband. "Please, Sahib, I wish to be your wife. I will be only yours. You are so handsome, like a Hindi star."

He stumbled past her down the stairs before he reached the sultry air of the alley and took a deep breath.

By a street light, he saw his white pants were smeared with pink powder like pollen from a filthy flowering tree. At home, he'd scrub himself head to foot, mercilessly scour his tainted flesh until he bled. The washerwoman Ravi could bleach the trousers clean. But no matter how he washed his body or his clothes, the consequences of his half hour with Usha wouldn't be cleansed away. He hadn't used protection, which meant he would have to postpone relations with his wife until he visited Dr. Fitzgerald. Anticipation of the examination and treatment made him feel sick. He vomited sour bile against a wall and wiped his mouth.

The little book in his pocket had lost all its charm. He was no scholar, no seeker of the truth, only a fantasist who made up stories to justify his corruption. He was no better than the hypocrite Brahmins exploiting a defenseless girl somewhere behind a dark temple.

He kept his head down, refusing to meet the eyes of men who passed in the alley. A European alone was prey for the gangs that roamed the docks. He had a terrible flashback of his night on the Jaffna waterfront, reminding him of the *Midnight Tiger* and the *White Sphinx*, the telegram not yet sent, of Ramachandra's sons involving him in risks.

He turned left when he reached Poonamallee High Road. Above the noise of the traffic, he heard a roaring in his head that he took at first for his own conscience, but when it stopped, then started up again, the frightful loud roar continued and he realized it came from the lonely old tiger in the Madras Zoological Gardens, so old he had become nearly hairless, a beast who showed himself only at night, roaring in fury at his fate, as Jules wished he could roar at his.

5.

Ravi the washerwoman stopped Celeste on the stairs to volunteer a marital commentary. "Sheets never soiled, not once," Ravi said, her red glass nose stud glittering.

"Do not gossip about Memsahib, not one word more." She glared at the small woman "I am going to her now. Is it that way?"

"Yes, Miss." Ravi raised an eyebrow toward a door, managing at the same time to wriggle her nose like a little rabbit. Celeste passed by her, surprised to be giving orders and having her authority respected.

"Come in." In the center of the room, a slender white arm and a delicate white hand stretched from the lacy coverlet on top of a wide bed. Celeste thought immediately of the *Soeurs* when they removed their coifs and revealed skin so white it seemed to have never been touched by the sun.

The rest of the Memsahib now emerged from under a muslin drape of mosquito netting gathered like skirts to let in a breeze. She was pale, with long black hair and blue eyes under which there were dark shadows.

"Hello, Celestine Celeste. My husband said you would come because I'm alone."

"My birth name is Celestine Marie, Memsahib, but here I am called Celeste."

"I'm Angela. No Memsahib. I don't like that."

"Miss Angela?"

"Angela is enough. Dr. Fitzgerald was here because I have caught something called Dengue fever. He was floating in whiskey and I'm glad he didn't come too close. You shouldn't either if I'm contagious."

"The Dengue fever came to Pondicherry every year, Miss, and I have had it. I nursed persons with the fever but I did not catch it."

"Did these person recover?" Angela asked.

"Oh yes."

"I'm so far away from my sister and mother and wish I could talk to them."

"The Sahib can arrange for a phone call."

"Probably, but right now I feel too weak even for that. I don't seem able to do anything but lie in bed. I have been a dancer, an active person who did barre exercises and took classes every day. It scares me that my muscles will go soft and I'll never get them back."

Celeste reached for the extended hand. "You will regain your health, Missy."

As she leaned behind Angela to plump the pillows, she felt the heat coming off the young woman's skin. On the pillow, strands of dark hair made a small nest like the beautiful red curls of Thérèse that had came out in handfuls after her fever.

That first morning, she did little but straighten the bed and help Angela into the bathroom where she washed. She dusted the several wardrobes and chests and re-arranged two chairs to face the window, so Angela could sit and look down on the garden below.

———

Two mornings a week Suddaraj arrived in the Sahib's car to pick up Celeste at the YWCA. He was a courteous young man, small and wiry, with a friendly smile she liked right away. He didn't try to be familiar as Ravi the washerwoman had, and he did not gossip. As soon as they arrived at the Sahib's, he brought her into the kitchen where he toasted slices of white bread, heated water for her tea, and arranged a plate of butter and jellies. When she asked him why he didn't eat, he replied, "I don't know if you will want to eat with me."

"Why should I not?"

"You are not Hindu?"

"No, I am Christian, why does that matter?"

"If you were Hindu, perhaps you would not wish to eat with me because I am unclean."

"You look entirely clean to me." She had noticed his pressed khaki shorts and shirt. "Why wouldn't I want to eat with you?"

"To a high caste Hindu, I am one who pollutes."

"I have heard of caste among the Hindus but I never met a person who suffered from how it is."

Suddaraj had to explain that he was born an Untouchable so that no matter what he did, nor how carefully he washed, he would still be unclean to higher castes and couldn't touch their food.

"How unfair that must be for you."

"I have known nothing else. We cannot change our birth in this life," he said.

"Still, it is unfair. I did not know my parents. I could have been born anything at all but fortunately those who raised me taught that we are all equal in God's eyes."

She looked up from her plate at this young man who accepted that his life was fixed and could not be changed, while she believed anything was possible.

A bell rang upstairs. They both jumped up and hurried to make a breakfast tray for Angela. Suddaraj arranged jasmine blossoms artfully around the plate of toast. A person who thought of pleasing another with flowers and spoke so honestly could never be unclean, Celeste decided.

Angela's fever had broken in the night and though she still seemed to radiate too much heat when Celeste arranged pillows behind her, she said she felt better.

"Thank you, Celeste. I'm famished all of a sudden. I feel better but I ache all over."

"We call the fever 'bone-breaker' because that is how it feels."

"I've had sore muscles before. I'll get over them. I'd like you to tell me about India."

"Oh, Miss, I've known only one place. Outside of Pondicherry, I feel like a stranger in a foreign country. Even this morning, I learned about unfair ways the people are being treated that I did not know, though I have lived in India all my life."

Celeste stood behind Angela, who sat with a towel over her shoulders in front of the mirror. Behind her, Salomé walked around, taking in the Memsahib's spacious and light bedroom, and then moved in to begin the hair cut.

"It's going to be so sweet." Salomé snipped and stood back. "You have fine hair, Mem."

Angela kept her eyes closed until she was told she could open them and look in the mirror.

"I'm so pale. I look like a ghost with a haircut. It's a good one, thank you."

"I hope you are satisfied with the styling, Miss." Salomé made a small curtsey but seemed to be waiting before leaving. Celeste knew the Sahib had already paid her but Salomé waited for a tip or a gift. She also knew her friend hated to leave all that she saw in the room, the white lacy bedcover and the canopy, the pretty bottles of scent and powder.

She took Salomé's arm and led her out of the room.

"You are rushing me."

They walked down the stairs and through the dark hallway where she kept Salomé from opening doors and peering into the many large and shuttered rooms.

"What a big home but so gloomy. This Memsahib has everything. The Sahib is handsome and must have lots of money. Do you receive gifts for being nice to him?"

"I am employed to help her. The Sahib is away."

Salomé tossed her braid. "When you are not talking from books and study, you are not so smart as I am, Celestine Marie. Oh, forgive me, Celeste. How are you liking the name?"

"I am becoming used to it."

When Celeste returned upstairs, Angela said, "What a pretty friend you have, but I'm glad you're here with me and not her. Did you know her in your convent?"

"Yes, like all of us, she was without family. Since she came to Madras she seems changed."

"Being such a pretty girl, she'll have opportunities but she needs to be careful."

"I agree, Missy. I worry because she has many desires for pretty things. "

"You observe everything. How have you learned to be so calm?"

She blushed. "I was encouraged, I suppose, to want to learn. This morning when Suddaraj told me of his life, I realized how ignorant I am. In Pondicherry, our minds were not enclosed by the walls but we met few who were not Christians like ourselves. "

"Life will be different for you and your friend, I think," Angela said.

───────────

At five, after her last manicure, Celeste was changing from her pink uniform into her skirt and blouse when Mr. Charles knocked on the dressing room door. "Come to speak with me."

In his office, Mr. Charles sat behind his desk while she stood.

"You come and go in cars. What are you doing with these people?" he asked.

"Sir, you agreed that I am to be helping Sahib Jules and Kamala Kumari. You gave permission to go to them before and after the hours I work here."

"I thought that nonsense would soon be over. The girls are not happy. The salon is always talking about you."

"Have you received complaints about my work? I have not been late, not one time."

"It's your coming and going that's upsetting, like some film person yourself. I think that cine woman is a bad influence. Either you are here or there, Miss, you must make up your mind."

She took a deep breath. "You have given me opportunity, Mr. Charles. I believe I have not disappointed."

"Does that mean you will not obey me and give up the other employment, Miss?"

"I'm sorry for any difficulty I am causing, Sir." She lowered her gaze.

Mr. Charles stood up and puffed out his chest in his uniform. "You can go. This week you have bookings, but I am giving warning, Miss. Your attitude will not be tolerated. I am tempted also to dismiss Miss Salomé, a strumpet in the making if ever I saw one. You French girls think you are better than the others."

"No, Sir. Salomé is a good worker, and everyone finds her pleasing. She has told me that you have been good to her. I am sure she is grateful."

"Do you think so?" he raised a thin eyebrow.

"Yes, definitely, Sir, my friend is very grateful."

"We'll see how grateful that one is."

As she left, she wondered if she should warn Salomé of trouble.

Angela was humming to herself and stretching her legs, holding onto the window sill for balance. Celeste thought her Missy's bare white calves looked as delicate as a child's but when she flexed them, taut muscles appeared. She said that her bones still ached and stretching helped.

The carillon from the girl's missionary college on the other side of the high wall played chimes on the quarter hour.

"I remember these hymns," Angela stretched forward and touched fingers to her toes.

"We sang them in French. Are you Catholic, Miss?"

"I was brought up a Baptist but I'm not anything now."

"That cannot be true. You must still love our blessed Mother." She herself could not imagine losing her love for the Virgin Mother who was always with her.

"I can accept the Mother better than the Father." Angela pointed up to the ceiling. "My own dad used his belt to impress commandments upon us. He was a hypocrite and a liar. When he left my mother, my sister, and me, I prayed he wouldn't ever come back. I'm sorry if that offends you. You may have wished to love the father you didn't know. My prayer was answered. He was gone."

"I have imagined my father was a ship's captain I was told drowned not long after I was born, but it may be only a story made up for me out of kindness. If you don't mind that I ask, would you tell me how you lived as a child?"

"My mother managed to support us, and beyond that, any money she could put aside went to dance lessons and ballet clothes for me. She kept nothing for herself and my sister suffered because she wasn't chosen the way I was, I mean, she didn't have a dancer's body or look. I got a lot of attention and everyone said I had a great future after I danced the Princess Aurora in *Sleeping Beauty* with the Los Angeles Ballet school production when I was fifteen. We had a selected audience of ballet aficionados and they all said I had a bright career ahead. Unfortunately, it was more or less downhill after my first and only Princess. I've been a disappointment to my teachers, and to myself."

"Why is that?" Celeste asked.

"Because I didn't fulfill the hopes my teachers and my mother had for me. I didn't fulfill my potential. I guess I was lucky when I was first noticed but I never took it for granted. I always worked hard." Angela looked at her feet, pointed her toes in their soft slippers.

"At first when I got to New York I had my chances and I kept telling my mother I was doing well even when I had audition after audition but no offer to join a ballet company. If you haven't made it in dance by twenty, you lose your confidence. By twenty, it's too late to break through in the classical repertoire. Modern dance can give you a longer life but you need a personal style. It's hard to explain, Celeste."

"How I would love to see a real ballet. I know princesses from picture books."

"There's magic that happens on stage, there really is. A little girl sitting in a theater when the lights go out sees beautiful dancers in white tulle float in the air but she doesn't know how scared we are we'll make a mistake, or how our feet are killing us. In those pretty pink slippers with satin ribbons, you have bloody toes all bandaged inside."

"That sounds painful, Missy."

"Being a dancer is pain that you feel privileged to suffer because it separates you from everyone else. There's a high you get when you perform and afterward you accept the pain in your feet. I will show you some ugly feet."

At that moment, Suddaraj entered with their tea tray, set down the silver pot and white china cups and a plate of biscuits.

"Would Memsahib like anything else?" he asked.

"Thank you, no."

When he left the room, Angela said, "My husband says Suddaraj is an exceptional person to have risen from his caste. I don't know about that, but I like him very much."

"I do, also. He's an honest person."

"I am fortunate to know both of you," Angela said. "I feel tired now."

———————

A week later, during their drive to College Road, Suddaraj brought up the subject of repairs that needed to be done to the house before the monsoon arrived. "Broken windows, and cracks must be stuffed against rats and snakes that enter when rains come, especially the rooms on the ground floor. Can you write for Sahib to have a list?"

"If you tell me what you think should be done, I will make a list," Celeste answered.

"I wish I could read, Baba. I had no chance for it but my eldest daughter is learning both reading and writing in a school for scheduled castes."

"You have a daughter of school age, Suddaraj? You seem so young."

"I am not sure of my birth date. I am twenty two or twenty three years. I have three daughters and a baby son named Ranga. My hope is that Lali my oldest will be a teacher one day."

"For me, reading was everything when I was growing up and I believe it gave me confidence to be taking chances now that I wouldn't otherwise. I will find Lali books."

"She is a modest girl but like you, she is improving herself."

"I will be pleased to help her. I am curious about the big rooms downstairs that never get opened. What are they used for? We need to open them and let in light."

"Servants in the college next to us say this house is haunted. You don't fear ghosts?"

"No, not in this house at least. How many years has Sahib lived in this house?"

"Two years only. He purchased for a good price, he told me."

"He's left so much to be done. Isn't that strange for a Sahib?"

"Yes, you are right, but Sahib is out of the city often, and before bringing the Memsahib Angela to the house, he often slept in one of his offices. There has been no woman to take care, that is the problem."

As Suddaraj parked the car, Celeste said, "Show me the downstairs please."

They stepped inside the first large room, dark with old drapes pulled. When her eyes were used to the dimness, Celeste saw plaster cracking off the roof and windows askew.

"I can see there is much to be done. What's in the back, in the garden? I've never been there but Missy and I hear birds and monkeys in the trees."

"Mr. Jules warns there are snakes, even cobras,"

"Then we must not go down there," Celeste said.

"I'll request Gopu to clear the garden. He is a snake charmer and will lead them away."

"Gopu? I know the man. He came to the film set with his snake." She remembered the cobra's hood rising for the sip of gin, and the old man who resembled his snake.

"Our first work will be getting Gopu. I will ask Sahib today," Suddaraj said.

––––––––––––

When Gopu arrived, the old man recognized Celeste.

"I don't see so well but I remember every voice and yours is sweet," he said.

"Will you remove snakes from the garden?" she asked.

The old man touched his turban and bowed. "You will stay inside and see them come."

Celeste, Angela, and Suddaraj stood together on the second-floor verandah looking down on the garden. At first they only heard Gopu playing his high pitched wind instrument. In moments, they saw a rustle in the thick undergrowth and watched in amazement as two dark, wriggling lines came closer to Gopu. Then a much larger snake, hood swaying like kelp rising on a wave, coiled and uncoiled until it came close to the basket Gopu had put out.

"Cobras? Is the old man not afraid they'll strike him?" Angela asked.

"He knows his business. Snakes will be gone," Suddaraj answered.

"I'll never set foot on those paths," Angela said.

"Nor I, Missy. It's good he's come so they don't enter the house."

"Don't worry, Memsahib and Baba, Gopu will have them all gone," Suddaraj said

By the end of an hour, at least five snakes had disappeared into Gopu's basket, for which Suddaraj paid him ten rupees per head.

6.

"Let me ask, why would a husband bring a wife to India if he didn't want to be with her?"

Angela and Celeste were walking on the shady side of College Road. Celeste knew this was a moment to tell Angela about her double employment, even though there was nothing significant in the fact that Kamala Kumari was formerly a friend of Sahib Jules. If she could find a way to say, 'I also am working for a cine actress. I believe your husband knew her,' then it would be off her mind. But since she did not want to convey gossip, Celeste saw no reason to repeat comments about the Sahib that girls made in the salon which Salomé had reported. Since it might only cause her Missy distress, Celeste put off mentioning the dancer.

"Soon you'll be up and going out to parties, Miss. Then Mr. Jules will take you many places with other Memsahibs." Celeste kept her eyes on the road, stepping over trash.

"Why should I be with other Memsahibs? Because of our skin color? Please don't think that I'm like the snobby British women. Jules doesn't like them himself." Angela paused. "I'm going to ask you a favor."

"Of course, Missy."

"I've told you dancers take pills for pains in our feet, our legs, our backs. There's no part of our body that doesn't hurt at some time. And not only the physical strain. We can't sleep so we take pills. In the morning, for confidence to go out and audition, you take something else. Pretty soon you don't even know why except you need the pills and you pay a lot of money for them. Can you understand?"

"Not very well, but I am listening."

They were approaching the noisy thoroughfare that went to Gemini Circle.

"Let's turn around, I'm getting tired and I want you to do something at home before I change my mind."

"Of course."

"Since I've been in India, because of the fever, I haven't taken pills. The doctor was surprised how long my fever lasted. He didn't ask questions or he'd have known I was detoxing."

"We gave you aspirin. What is detoxing, Miss?"

"De-toxing is getting drugs out of my body. I don't think I would have done it if I hadn't been so sick."

"You were ill for three weeks. Now you're getting strong again."

"I was addicted and three weeks have passed since I took anything."

As they let themselves in through the gate and approached the house, Celeste could hear the workmen sweeping up debris on the first floor. She didn't want to ask what Missy meant by the word addicted if anyone else were listening.

"Go in the bathroom, get every container of pills and flush them down the toilet. I'll wait down here until you say you've done it. All of them. I want to hear the water and the flush. Hurry."

Angela sat on a chair looking out the window while Celeste went into the bathroom, opened the cabinet, found the containers with capsules of different colors. She opened each bottle and tossed down the contents, then pulled the chain and watched them go down. Somewhere below there was a gurgle in the plumbing. She hoped nothing would come back up.

"Missy, I have done it."

"Make some kind of sign of the cross or whatever you do to mark this moment, then come give me a hug."

Celeste stared at the empty toilet bowl. Why should she cross herself?

"Did they all go down?" Angela asked.

"Yes, Missy, all gone."

"Come on, give me a hug. You don't know what this means.

Whatever happens now, I've made a new start. Maybe Jules knew what he was doing bringing me here without realizing it. Life works in mysterious ways. Do you want to know about the pills?"

"No, I think I understand. You don't need them any longer."

"I think that's true. I hope so."

"Where did you meet the Sahib, Missy?" Celeste asked when they were seated in front of the window looking down on the garden.

"In New York, where I lived. Do you want to hear about our courtship?"

"Yes, of course. I am very fond of love stories."

"You'll decide if you call it a love story. Sit here." Angela patted the stair beside her. "We can play hooky for the afternoon."

"What does hooky mean, Missy?"

"Hooky? To avoid work, or school. Maybe we should look at the rooms that you're undertaking to clean up. I haven't seen them."

They walked down the stairs and entered one of two large rooms facing each other with wide doors. The workmen had moved furniture to the center of the rooms and covered everything to protect it from the dust of scraping away paint and patching holes.

"This is a ballroom. Celeste, my dear, let me lead you across the floor in a quadrille. I do know a great number of court dances, entirely useless except in fanciful conditions like this."

"I cannot dance, Missy."

"We all can, it's natural. Animals dance when they court. All creatures dance."

Angela placed a left hand behind Celeste's waist and took her right in her own. "Just follow me, side by side. First we curtsey to our partner."

Suddaraj watched the Memsahib turn Baba around the room until they all began laughing so hard they sat on the floor.

"Is this how you were dancing when Sahib saw you?"

"Oh, no, it was a performance on a stage. I was wearing such a sheer yellow dress He said I floated like a sunbeam. Quite poetic."

"The dress you were wearing was a ballerina costume?"

"No, this was modern dance, no tutus, no princesses or plot exactly but there was an implied emotional story line because our director Tomas revered Anthony Tudor. In the first dance, Tomas cast me as the ingénue, a young girl on the verge of life. It was the best role I'd had since Princess Aurora. Honestly, Celeste, the three years in New York, I'd lost something, confidence, drive, all the things you have to have even more than talent. I'd been drifting. I wouldn't say letting myself go, but not keeping peak, which means falling behind. Tomas gave me a chance and I was not going to let it go."

Celeste listened, nodding and understanding enough without knowing anything dance. What she knew was you had to want to improve yourself or you would just drift, as her Missy said.

"I got a lot of applause and calls to come back and be acknowledged. It felt wonderful. During the intermission, I went outside to the courtyard behind the church where we were performing. Quite a few dancers were out there for a smoke. I didn't smoke. I just wanted to take in the moment. The cool stones felt good on my feet." Angela brought her knees to her chest.

"A man was there, sitting on the steps. He smiled, then he stood up and bowed. What a gentleman, I thought, probably the father of one of the dancers. I remember wishing I had someone come to watch me. He said hello so politely and asked if I wanted privacy. He had an accent."

"Mr. Jules speaks perfectly."

"Yes, you guessed. He praised me and said I'd danced from my eyebrows to my fingertips. Then I had to get back inside. I blew him a kiss."

Angela stood and began walking back and forth moving her arms above her, twirling around the floor. "He gave me inspiration for the second half. I didn't have such a big part but I felt light and strong. I knew that I had all eyes on me but I didn't let anything take away my focus. I wanted to talk to the stranger afterward to thank him. I was afraid he would be gone with one of the dancers by the time I changed but he was waiting outside the church after everyone left. He asked if I'd have dinner with him. Usually I don't go out with a man I don't know but he seemed so cultivated and I was always glad for a meal. He took me to a French restaurant, really expensive. I loved it."

"French!" Celeste felt a wave of longing. "Did you have the

Crèpes Suzette? I read about them, with the flames coming off. I wonder how they taste."

"You know, I did have crèpes. My first time. They melted in my mouth. We talked about Holland, his travels, and India. I'd heard of Indian dance but I didn't know the first thing about it. I told him how hard it was in New York, how Tadeus, the director, and this little company were a godsend but the run was only three weekends and then I wasn't sure what I'd do."

Angela paused. "He reassured me I was very good and that he was sure that I needn't worry. He encouraged me like the good father I didn't have. I felt happy."

Celeste listened, still imagining the Crèpes Suzettes and hoping to hear more about them.

"He was in and out of New York for business and I didn't see him all week, but he came to the performance with flowers the next Friday. We had dinner again, and the next night. Frankly, I didn't know what he was after. He never kissed me or made a pass. I began to wonder if maybe he was gay, or just an older lonely guy on a trip by himself to the States."

"Mr. Jules is more quiet than gay."

"The gay I mean is homosexual, that he likes men."

Celeste averted her eyes.

"So many dancers and balletomanes are gay. They can be a girl's best friend."

"Oh," she said.

"Oh, is right, especially if you like someone and it turns out they're gay. It happens all the time. The nicest men. Anyway, the night of our last performance, he said he had to leave for London the next morning. I couldn't go to the airport because my day job was waitressing breakfast and lunch on Madison Avenue but by the time I got back to my apartment, a bouquet of roses and a box of chocolates were waiting with a note. 'Thank you for beautiful nights. I will always remember your yellow dress and our conversations.'"

"I do not believe it is true that Mr. Jules prefers men, as you say."

"I guess that's true but when you hear the rest, you'll know why

I think it might be a possibility. Anyway, I felt protected and cared for when he was around. I didn't know him well though we'd talked a lot, mostly about me. There aren't many men who listen. Then things kind of fell apart for me. Tadeus was offered a teaching gig at a college in the Midwest. He called us in, we all had a good cry and went home. I felt as though I'd lost my family." Angela paused, staring at her feet. "I proceeded to do a stupid thing. I'm afraid to tell you about it. I feel sick to my stomach just remembering."

"Missy, I'm sorry you had no one to comfort you."

Angela turned away from Celeste's eyes. "I took pills and drank vodka, which is a very bad combination. At the same time, Jules was flying back from London. Why my timing was so perfect has to be fate, it really does. He had a feeling, an intuition, he said, and he got a flight back to New York. When I didn't answer the door, he called the super who let him in. I was lying on the couch. He knew something was wrong. He made me throw up, and walk and drink coffee. He said I had to come with him, that I'd find a refuge for a time in India. He took charge of everything. I got vaccinations and a passport. I'd never had a passport."

Angela turned her gold band on her finger. "Then we got married."

"Married in a church?" Celeste was still puzzling over what Angela said about vodka and pills and what they might cause to happen.

"We went to City Hall. He bought me a spray of orchids and lovely clothes for travel. He chose everything. He was going to take care of me. This is almost up to the present. The fever and months here and hardly seeing him, I wonder what kind of mistake we made and if he regrets it. He doesn't touch me, Celeste. He hasn't ever, not once."

Celeste remembered Ravi's words about the untouched sheets. What could she say to Missy? That Sahib was being a gentleman because she'd been sick and perhaps he was trying to avoid catching the fever himself?

"Why do I make such bad decisions, one after another? Except for today, getting rid of the pills."

7.

"Poor thing. What does the wife wear when she goes out? Sad little frocks?" Kamala asked as they drank coffee on the bungalow verandah that faced the beach where surf crashed and tumbled up the flat sandy shore. The monsoon was approaching and the roiled-up sea was giving warning to stay far from it.

"What lovely sounds the sea makes, even now," Kamala said.

"Not to me. I am afraid of it," Celeste replied. "In Pondicherry, during monsoon, people were swept off the esplanade by giant waves. And the story La Mère told of my mother and father perishing in a storm has never left me."

Kamala paced from the windows and back, listening closely to Celeste's account of the sea captain and his princess wife perishing in the monsoon. "I know it is a fairy story but I will never know anything more about myself so perhaps a story is better than nothing."

"We are at the mercy of the stars although some unfortunate persons disregard warnings. Just as you must be wary of the sea, my astrologer continues to see a danger from a man who wears a uniform. Now tell me more about the person whose name I do not want to hear."

Celeste thought of what detail she could give that wouldn't be disloyal.

"She doesn't wear frocks. Ahmed finished several *shalwar kamise* for her to wear to meet the Memsahibs for supper."

"Ahmedji, *my* tailor! Do not tell me he is dressing her!" Kamala's eyes turned smoky and her mood of friendly conversation seemed to vanish. "It is a sword to my heart to hear his treachery. I will cut

Ahmed dead when he comes looking for business from me. He must choose. Kamala Kumari is not a customer to be trifled with. The hundreds and hundreds of rupees I have paid him! Even on the covers of film magazines I have worn his *shalwar kamise*. The man should show gratitude. Next you will tell me that I'm sharing my jeweler."

She recoiled at the vehemence in Kamala's voice.

"No. Missy wears only small pearls in her ears, nothing to draw attention."

"I suppose a small person would not wear necklaces, though they suit my long neck."

"She's not overly tall, you are correct."

Kamala seemed somewhat placated by the description. She circled the orchids, gardenias, and bougainvillea blooming in pots, plucked dead flowers and crushed them between her nails and her palm before throwing them over the railing and onto the sand below.

"The Madras Club is dull and the food tasteless, so let him take her there. What else did the American tell you about the British club?"

"She said the dessert was called *Divine Pavlova*."

"*Pavlova* without me! *Divine Pavlova*! It is our dessert!" Kamala twisted her sari and began tearing shiny leaves from a banana tree. "She'll know soon enough he cannot control himself with other women. You may tell her that."

"Lately, Sahib encourages her to ride horses with the British ladies."

"Ah, at last, now you have said what proves to me he doesn't love her. He would never have let me go near to a horse. I prefer *Pèche Melba* and won't touch *Pavlova* again." Kamala's thick black eyebrows furrowed above her nose and her eyes seem to burn.

Celeste felt saved from making further mistakes by the telephone ringing. She picked up the receiver and brought the phone to Kamala on the terrace.

"Come soon, my dear…tonight," she said into the receiver, then returned the phone to its cradle. "Run my bath, Celeste."

In the bathroom, Celeste turned the gold-plated faucets that Kamala ordered from Singapore. Perfume bottles lined the shelves as well as English and French soaps carved into pretty flowers. How Salomé would like to have these pretty things, Celeste thought for a moment as the warm water flowed in. She poured in powder that made fragrant bubbles.

"The bath is ready," she called.

Kamala dropped her towel and stepped in, washing her feet and making motions of sudsing before calling for a towel. In Celeste's opinion, this hardly constituted a real wash. At the convent, they had no perfumed soaps but much scrubbing.

Kamala was still dressing when the doorbell rang. Celeste opened the door to let in Hari Laksman, a giant of a man who towered above her. Not only his size and bulk made her step away and let him pass at a distance but he had a rough face with scars on his cheeks, the way the pirate had been made up for Kamala's film.

Kamala swept into the room, stood on tiptoes and kissed Hari, and then they left without saying anything to each other.

From the window, she noticed that the man did not open her door as Mr. Jules always did for a woman. He was no gentleman but Kamala appeared to be happy with him. Celeste shook her head, unable to imagine where they were going and what they would be doing. She returned to the bath, scrubbed the rim, ran more hot water, added additional bubbling powder and slipped in for a long soak away from people and their troubles.

When Kamala Kumari met Hari Laksman at a Gemini Studios reception, his broad shoulders and jutting profile made her think he was a Bombay actor or producer. She made herself easy to talk to, standing close to him, her small full figure tightly wrapped in a peacock blue sari. From the moment he spoke, she realized that he was not a director nor actor but a businessman, and not very bright. He saw few films. Kamala decided that even though there wouldn't be much to talk about, his physique attracted her and she gave him her telephone number. Jules had left after they'd argued and she hadn't heard a word from him. She certainly would not give him the pleasure of thinking she wouldn't enjoy the company of another man. When Hari did not call, she got in touch with him.

Hari Laksman lived in a household of women that included his widowed mother and her sister, his wife and a female cousin, all Sikhs from parts of the Punjab that had been turned over to Pakistan during the Partition of India. In the violence that had swept the country, Hari, only a boy, remembered his mother carrying him from their burning home to the railway station where his father and other village men thrust the women and children into train carriages, then lined up with their farm tools to hold off the armed Mohammedans until the train left the platform. No one ever saw these men again.

When the train with the wounded and terrified Sikhs finally arrived in New Delhi, Hari no longer spoke a word. A cousin with a bicycle repair shop taught him to hold tires to a flame so the patches would adhere. With time, he recovered his speech.

Hari went from repairing tires to managing small shops until Hind Tires Ltd. in New Delhi hired him to manage a plant. His transfer to Madras as sub-director of the southern region was a move up but he and his family missed the north. He'd been a loyal husband until the afternoon he met Kamala Kumari at Gemini Studios; she made certain that he knew what she wanted but he hesitated. A week later, Kamala called him to accompany her to the Apsara Inn on the outskirts of Madras.

Tonight, the graceful Assamese girl, Sita, welcomed back Kamala and Hari at the door of the Apsara before the brothel owner, a 250-pound Punjabi woman named Muma Devi, waddled into the reception room and embraced Kamala. They complimented each other on health and fortune and went off for a moment's private conversation about arrangements for the evening.

"You are wise to be rid of that Dutchman who was only trouble to you. Your new beloved is welcome here. You shall have the second suite," Muma said.

Jules and the obese madam had disliked each other but Muma

approved of Hari who had said a few words complimenting her on the décor which was her passion.

Muma loved the *Belle Époque*, Paris at the end of the century, the French pleasure houses she tried to replicate in the Nabob's old palace. She had curtained the downstairs in red velvet with *fleur de lys* and hung the rooms with chandeliers. A recording of *La Bohème* had worn scratchy from the times she played it.

She designed the second-floor rooms in contrast to the drapery and opulence of the downstairs reception, leaving them unfurnished except for beds and washbasins. These rooms Muma called her *sanctums* because they were intended for a special clientele, the Brahmin judge or the religious Chettiyar businessman, who took their illicit pleasures as if they were entering *Devadasi* quarters behind a village temple. Muma understood that such upper-caste men had to perform various rituals of purification before they returned to their wives, washing out their mouths and privates, praying to Siva or Vishnu that their bodies polluted from lying with unclean women would be cleansed again by the water. For this, Muma left water conveniently in basins.

The top, third floor of the former palace served the voluptuaries, Mohammedans, Parsis, Europeans, and Chinese without religious compunctions. The most beautiful and talented girls Muma employed entertained in suites furnished with satin and decorated with erotic art. Here was where Kamala led Hari.

"Not yet, dear. We'll drink a little now we're settled." Kamala saw that teaching this bull of a man patience would be worth her time. She poured him beer and a gin for herself. After they drank, she rubbed his ankles, moved her fingers up his firm calf muscles, around his knees, to his thick thighs. Beneath the fragrance of his cologne, he smelled faintly of petroleum and tar in his thick pubic hair. She removed his shirt and felt a strange thrill pressing her fingers to the shiny lines of scar tissue, scars that had grown with him and become particularly erotic to her when he told her of the desperate escape from the armed Mohammedans many years back

"'My love,' she sang. 'Come to me, I can no longer bear the anguish of desire.' This is how Radha sings to Krishna, as the god makes her wait."

But Hari had waited long enough. He lifted Kamala until her small body lay upon him in just the right position for a woman of her height to be best held by a tall man. She scissored her legs around his waist as she sucked his lips and explored inside his mouth with her tongue. The *bindi* spot in her forehead felt on fire. "Take me, take me," she moaned.

He pressed her back into the pillows and filled her completely, yet Kamala urged him further, looking into his huge black pupils, before she gave herself up to the waves that traveled up her spine, becoming pinwheels of fire behind her eyes. "My giant, my god," she cried out.

The miracle of this man was that he had more in him. After they made love, rather than being diminished, his erection almost instantly rose again as Kamala stretched herself around him. This time her body was even more on fire when her orgasm came, colored lights spinning and firing her nerves. Was this satisfaction not more to her liking than love itself could ever be? Was she not better to be finally free of the entanglement with Jules that brought her so little pleasure and so much anger? Yet she could not get the image of his face from her mind as she fell asleep.

Late at night, Kamala circled the small of Hari's back with her moist fingers, awakening him. She rubbed her nipples on his scars, lightly pinched his chest, rocking over him until she covered his penis with her vulva and he was again inside her.

The open windows let in a breeze that cooled their heated skin. Prayer music rose from the rooms below where a recording of Subbulakshmi implored Sri Krishna to "Come, come my Lord, you are my Lord, my love." Kamala sang the verse to Hari but he slept without moving.

Hours later, slender lemon-scented Sita brought coffee thick with sugar and a plate of mangoes. Sita didn't seem an intruder on their intimacy, more like an appreciative witness of their ardor, watching as Kamala fed Hari slippery peppered mango slices and sucked them from his mouth.

8.

"Wait, please, Madams!" The British women pushed Celeste aside, waving their arms at her to get out of the way, like a flock of hens, she thought. There were four Memsahibs, two dressed alike in breeches ballooning out behind their wide behinds. Their faces both had an identical cabbage look. A third Memsahib, red-headed and flushed, was also broad, while the fourth, stringy and brown-skinned, led the charge.

They halted to look at the construction mess on the ground floor. "Oh, my god," exclaimed the stringy Memsahib, tilting her head upward, then scanning the broken plaster and boards that were lying where workmen left them. "I've never seen such a disaster. How does one live here?"

Celeste ran ahead up the stairs to warn Angela. "Memsahibs coming up."

"I met them at the club," Angela said.

"There is a red-haired one, a thin one, and twins, I believe."

"That's them. They asked me to go riding at the beach, but since we didn't make a date, I thought they'd forget. I don't think they liked me, but they're curious how I live. They're probably snooping downstairs. I hope they get an eyeful to gossip about."

She saw a smile on Angela's face and felt more confident.

"Shall I say you are not well?"

"That's just putting them off. Actually, I'll enjoy a ride. One of the few good things I remember about my father is that he got my sister and me into the saddle early. We didn't dare be afraid of the horses—he was scarier than they ever were. I stopped riding when

64

I started dance lessons because the teacher said it bowed your legs, but you don't forget how, like swimming."

"I would never learn swimming, Missy. And I will be afraid of horses as well if I come close to them. Are you sure you want them to come up?"

"Let them come, we'll be fine."

The thin Memsahib with leather skin and a stick she slapped against her breeches climbed the stairs. Celeste backed up as they strode in.

"It's not so bad here, but downstairs, it's rubble," said the thin woman.

"There's a crew at work," Angela said. "The house has been neglected a long time."

"Centuries, by the look. The mildew itself—whew. Bleach everything, that's what it needs. Do you remember my name, by the way? I'm Pamela."

"Pamela, I remember. You were the one telling me what not to do at the Club."

"Someone has to take the newcomer in hand. We're easy to get on with if you follow the rules. After we ride, we'll make plans for you."

"I don't have riding breeches. And I haven't followed rules for most of my life."

"We can go home and get her some breeches," the red-headed woman said.

"Too much trouble. She's got to have something that will do."

To Celeste's surprise, Pamela began rummaging in Angela's wardrobe. She pulled out a loose pair of cotton pants. "These will do for now. What are they for anyway?"

"Dance workout, relaxing."

"Oriental, like a native. We'll find you a proper pair. Let's go." Pamela said.

"They don't want me, Missy," Celeste whispered to Angela who whispered back, "I need you, please come."

Celeste slipped into the front seat beside the driver. Angela sat down beside her.

"No, you ride back with us, not in front with the servant," Pamela ordered.

"You need the room back there," Angela answered.

Celeste had no experience with animals except kittens left on the Convent doorstep, as she'd been left, in a box. Dogs in the streets were sick and mangy, covered in flies, without a home. Cows had roamed less frequently in Pondicherry than Madras where they made even buses lurch and screech to a halt. This horse, the one they were going to put her Missy on, was a huge creature blowing steam from its nostrils like an engine. One small man was holding the huge head and the other lifted Angela's foot to a platform and then boosted her onto the saddle. She felt afraid but her Missy seemed calm enough to pat the shining wet side of the horse and lean down to whisper to it. The animals' ears went back as if listening.

The last Celeste saw of her, Angela was last in the line of Memsahibs riding out from the stable. Seated on the horse, she thought her mistress looked like a child.

She spent the next hour between a torment of imagined disasters and the real misery of being attacked by big flies. Finally she heard hooves pound on the packed dirt of the stable path. Angela arrived alone, her short black hair wet and in her eyes. The large black horse panted and came to a halt.

"Missy, are you hurt?" Celeste approached as close as she dared.

"No, but someone else might have been. I'll just walk this big guy around to cool down. Would you call for the groom?"

The two men who'd put Angela on the horse came forward to hold its head as she got down.

"What happened, Missy?"

"Pamela, that obnoxious bully, the one bossing the rest of them, came up behind and spurred my horse on. I don't know why she did it, maybe to scare me. This guy took off and ran until I let him tire himself out. There was nothing in our way, just miles of sand and we both loved it, this big guy and I, but that woman is a real troublemaker."

Just then, Pamela came trotting up on her white mare.

"What were you doing rushing up behind me?" Angela held Pamela's mount by its rein.

"I should have told you that my mare is used to being first."

"That's right, you should have, Pamela."

"Are you accusing me of intentionally making your horse run off?"

"I had control and could have stopped whenever I wanted but you didn't know that. You thought I was a novice. What is wrong with your thinking, Pamela?"

'How dare you!' Pamela flicked her stick close to Angela's hands.

"Missy, come out of the sun," Celeste called.

"Will you be still, girl! Scat!" Pamela flicked her stick with its whip end in the air toward Celeste.

In a second, Angela had the whip in her hands and was holding it in Pamela's face.

"How dare you threaten Celeste?"

"Celeste! That is quite some name for a servant," Pamela sputtered.

The rest of the Memsahibs cantered into a circle around Angela and Pamela.

"We will go home, Celeste," Angela said.

The three other women dismounted and stayed close together without speaking. Even Pamela was silent until Angela again slid in the front seat in beside Celeste.

Pamela leaned forward and tapped Angela's shoulder.

"Sitting with your servant. Word will get out. Driver," Pamela tapped the driver.

"Driver, please go on, we want to get home," Angela said.

"Pamela, dear, calm down, we'll be there soon," said Virginia, the red-headed woman.

They reached College Road and slowed to turn in at Angela's compound. When they stopped, Virginia leaned forward. "Don't forget, you're coming for a swim at the Club."

"I don't think we will," Angela stepped out of the car, then waited until Celeste got out and shut the door.

"But I want you to!" Virginia held Angela's arm. "We don't want to end the day this way. I'd like you to be my guest, please!"

"All right, Virginia. A swim will be nice. We'll come with our driver, Mr. Suddaraj."

Suddaraj looked from Angela to the young woman he affectionately called Baba.

"I am ready for that cool shower you've been installing." Angela wiped dirt from her hands onto a towel Suddaraj gave her.

"Why did you say you would go for swimming?" Celeste followed Angela upstairs. "That nasty brown woman might try to harm you again."

"I'm not ready to let her have her way. It's been quite a day so far, hasn't it? We might as well carry on with this until the end. If I've been bored, now I'm not."

"Thank you for defending me, Missy. I don't know what to say to those Memsahibs."

"No problem. I just find they're an embarrassment. They don't bother me at all."

The sun was still burning hot and Celeste felt relieved that she didn't have to leave the shadows of the verandah at the Madras Club. She wasn't exactly hiding but she put herself as far from sight as possible after fetching her own chair and pulling it into the shade. At least no one objected to her being here, she thought. Just another servant.

A dozen or more Memsahibs and several fair-skinned Indian matrons were playing cards inside the chilly clubhouse while dark-skinned Indian women watched little children. Five Memsahibs, including Angela, clustered around the pool. She was glad that Angela wore the modest swimming costume they had bought at Spencer's Emporium even though she'd laughed at it and said she'd never worn such an ugly suit. "With a skirt!"

The twins and Virginia with her red hair seemed unconcerned exposing pinkish mottled flesh to the sun. Pamela, more wrinkled and skinny than anyone around her, seemed to be without shame—otherwise, how could she wear two pieces of cloth and look like a dressed-up lizard?

Their voices carried up from the pool. "I fell madly in love with Douglas at first sight," she heard Virginia say. "I've never stopped going all weak when I see him. He looked like Robert Taylor in *Waterloo Bridge*."

Celeste thought Angela seemed to favor this Virginia. She spoke only to her not the others. "I loved *Waterloo Bridge*. Vivien Leigh was a ballerina before she became an actress. I'd like Celeste to see it."

"You're not talking about that ridiculous Anglo Indian servant?" Pamela's voice was shrill.

"She's French actually."

"French via Africa. Dark as they come. You are making a sorry fool of yourself whether you realize it or not," Pamela said.

"I might as well take a dip," Angela said.

She watched as Angela swam to the end of the pool and back. When she climbed out, she shook water onto Pamela.

"What the hell!" Pamela stuttered.

"I enjoyed that swim. I feel refreshed. Now I think Celeste and I will go."

"A real Indian-lover." Pamela stood up and faced Angela. "Your husband, the Dutchman, is an Indian-lover, too, mixed up in things. You'll find out soon enough. My husband knows quite a lot. So do the police. They keep tabs on men like him."

Suddaraj ran forward with an umbrella when he saw them.

"Where can you take us that will be cool and shady?" Angela asked.

"Museum is cool, Madam," Suddaraj said. "Sahib often goes to the museum."

"Then take us there, thank you. You know, I dislike snobbishness and ignorance and I'm sorry if they hurt your feelings, Celeste. We won't bother to see them again, one day was enough."

"Sometimes even the *Soeurs* reminded us we were Indians and they came from France."

"That's too bad," Angela said.

"They meant no harm. They missed their home," Celeste replied.

"You have a more generous nature than I do," Angela said.

Suddaraj turned onto a gravel lane and stopped the car before a pinkish-red building. Feathery flamboyant blossoms shaded the entrance. "Here is the museum, Memsahib."

No one appeared in the entry hall to sell them tickets, so they walked through into a shaded garden. Celeste, who had seen religious pictures, images of statues of Jesus unclothed in the Virgin's arms, was not prepared for the nakedness of life-size men and women in the museum. They were standing so casually it looked as if they were conversing. Her eyes followed curlicues of light up a woman's arms to her breasts. She kept from looking at the male figure who was a head taller than the female and had private parts exposed for anyone to see.

In a gesture that took her entirely by surprise, Suddaraj slipped one hand over the breast of a woman made of bronze. Celeste crossed her arms over her chest as if she might need to protect herself.

"Suddaraj has probably never been in a museum before," Angela whispered. "He doesn't know that you're not allowed to touch. But no one is watching and aren't they beautiful! Really so graceful. What a relief from the awful Brits."

"She is Parvati, our little mother, Lord Siva's wife. She is leading her husband to the divine couch." Suddaraj walked to the side of another goddess whose haunch tilted toward them.

"Do not misunderstand my meaning, Memsahib and Baba. It is devotion to the mother of life we Hindus feel. We honor sisters, wives, all women who bring us from their bodies, nourish us from their breasts, giving us life."

Celeste wiped her face. "It is not our way to respect the Mother."

9.

Kamala Kumari stood admiring duty-free bottles of scotch and gin lined up on the dresser in the professor's room in the Connemara Hotel.

"May I offer you a drink?" Dr. Francis Standard leaned closer to the table to read the labels. "There appears to be gin and whiskey."

"I admire Queen Victoria more every time I see her head on the bottle." Kamala tucked her orange sari with green borders tightly around her hips. "We lack opportunities, as far as drink is concerned. We depend upon friends to arrive from abroad bringing us gifts."

"Do you prefer lemon squash or tonic? And it is gin you wish?" he asked.

"Squash, only a splash. Yes, gin is what I prefer."

Kamala inhaled the juniper berry fragrance of gin. "You will drink a glass with me?"

"It's early in the day," he answered.

"As long as you avoid ice, no harm will come. A friend told me that gin came from his native Netherlands and is medicinal." She drank. "I received your invitation to discuss the possibility of performing in America. Of course, I have other engagements to consider."

"The Orient Foundation is eager to sponsor your visit, Miss Kumari. Since Tanjore Balasarawati's first appearances in America and at festivals, there has been a great interest in your art. We will plan the performances and class demonstrations, culminating with an evening in New York at our Friends Foundation. We'll handle publicity and you will receive an honorarium of $5,000 for two weeks, as well as all travel expenses and hotel arrangements. Friends of Indian culture and music may never have seen a performance of *bharatanatyam* by a true practitioner of classical South Indian dance who is also a film star. You will draw audiences everywhere you go."

"Thank you. That is generous of you. I know what success my cousin Balasaraswati had when she visited America and I am honored that our art is appreciated in the United States as it often is not here in India where people wish to see cinema dancing, though I cannot complain."

Kamala fanned herself with the fringe of her sari and looked sideways to examine more closely the odd man before her. The way his thin neck rose above his white collar made him look a bird, and the odd little tuft of blondish hair growing downward from his chin, the same straw color and dry texture of his hair, was birdlike also. He had greenish eyes behind glasses.

"The Foundation plans to publish a monograph on your art and culture to accompany your tour. The author we have been in touch with is the man who recommended I speak to you. He didn't say if you were acquainted but I suppose you know Mr. Van Steen who lives here in Madras, a true devotee of classical music and dance. From him I have learned of your noble lineage, one of the last *Devadasis* to have been dedicated in a temple before it was outlawed. Truthfully, I am awestruck to meet an actual practitioner of this art."

He sat back and smiled at her but Kamala felt as if she'd been hit by a blow that took all the air from her lungs. She'd been intrigued that an American professor wanted to meet her. Now it made sense. Jules was up to some kind of trick to humiliate her by making this chicken-neck of a man tempt her with an offer hard to refuse, a trip to America, all expenses paid and $5,000 on top of that, at the cost of revealing what he knew she did everything to conceal.

"Van Steen believes his study will be a revelation on the origins of the sacred and profane in religious practice," the chicken-neck continued.

She took a deep sip from her glass to give herself time. Noble lineage and musical inheritance! To these men, she was something exotic, like a rare animal in a cage to be exhibited by them. They knew so little that she wanted to laugh, but the chance to display her talents in America, to put herself ahead of Shanti, even Malini! She poured more Queen Victoria. She would throw this professor a few crumbs.

"Professor, you're aware that India banned dedication of young girls to Hindu temples to save them from very bad lives."

Dr. Standard cleared his throat. "I do know of the duality of your caste."

Duality! He sounded like Jules himself. She'd shock this man right out of his collar.

"Even up to my grandmother's time, we women depended on the temple for rice and clothing, and sometimes jewels, in exchange for performances and duties required by our religion. We were poor as you cannot imagine. My mother was a beautiful woman who died at only thirty two years of age from tuberculosis, a disease many contracted because of the unsanitary conditions we lived in. We were badly used by men of high caste, if you understand my meaning."

Kamala drank a large swallow.

"Please understand. I am an actress whose reputation is most important to my career. The past is better left alone. There are still bad words used in speaking of our caste."

Did she dare say them? The gin gave her courage. "Prostitute, temple whore," she said.

The man's face paled even more over his white shirt. "In my travels, I've found that speaking to an informant of their past, the rituals and rules that were followed, can be liberating. Being a temple dancer is a heritage of which to be proud."

"Are we rare animals viewed by the public as curiosity?" she asked.

"You are a treasure I hope to bring to the world."

I will give him a chance, she thought. He is offering me too much to lose.

"To us, children, especially girls, temples were frightening places. In these dark quarters, priests and their Brahmin friends, old and ugly men, mistreated girls of my caste. Many contracted venereal disease. I saw terrible deaths."

"I am sorry to hear that," Standard said.

Kamala brushed away his remarks with a wave of her hand. "One day I shall write a movie script about the real life of *Dasis*, not the happy *nautch* dancers I myself have acted." She reached for the gin bottle again, then looked at the Professor who seemed at a loss.

"The public knows Kamala Kumari as a Gemini artist. The studio has created a biography that never mentions caste. Van Steen speaks without my permission."

"I am listening to you, Miss Kumari. Your words matter to me."

"Grandmother determined to marry me as was customary in our caste to the deity of the temple even though by then the law prohibiting the practice had passed, but she followed the old ways."

Kamala felt giddy from the gin on an empty stomach, from being so high up in a room above the skyline of Mount Road. This man wanted to know more. Should she trust him? She poured half a glass of Victoria.

My cousin Pattu and I," she said softly, "had no suspicions the night Grandmother dressed us in new skirts and *cholis*. She was usually harsh, but that day she gave us sweets and a ball to play with. Ordinarily, we had no toys, no games. Our life was learning dance and we knew no other children to compare ourselves with. Pattu was nine and I was ten, but she was taller, with fair skin, a round face, a pleasant disposition. She is still a more gentle person. She found a husband who keeps her in comfort. I was the difficult one who showed the most talent and temperament, so I received more beatings from the teacher. Nor have I settled as Pattu has done. My nature is restless."

The professor had pulled a notepad out and was quickly scribbling. Should she stop now? Or let this stranger report back to Jules?

"I will give you a description of the dedication that is accurate but you will not use my name. My name must not appear anywhere."

The professor nodded. "I will honor your wishes."

"Imagine two young girls led into a dark temple with light only kerosene lamps provide. They are told to stand upon a pile of unhusked rice covered by a golden cloth. The god icon, Sivalingum, looms above. You know, this god is a man's organ, his penis."

She waited for the color to rise again from the professor's neck to his ears.

"So now an old woman, a grandmother like mine, lifts one girl's foot up and places it upon the rice while the priest ties a *tali* around her neck. *Talis* are like your wedding rings, the sign of a marriage. Pattu and I are now brides of the Lord Siva. Priests are chanting prayers as we are taken to visit men who congratulate us on our wedding. They are rich men and they are going to wait until we are a few years older to become our husbands. I imagine, Professor, that if you have a daughter, you would not want this to happen to her."

The professor was keeping his head down over his notebook. "There are practices that today we find difficult to accept," he said.

"They were not easy to accept at that time," Kamala said.

"I have two girls," he said. "I'm protective of them. I understand your point."

Kamala reached for the bottle that had become lighter. She was ashamed to have let the drink talk, felt a shame that never entirely left her free of its weight.

"Did you know that Anna Pavlova visited India?" Kamala asked.

"I did not know that, but it is a coincidence that Mr. Van Steen's mother, as he's told me, danced with the ballerina long ago."

"Oh yes? Well, that is not what I'm speaking of. Anna Pavlova praised the greatness of our temple dance. She believed in reincarnation and has said that in a former life she herself may have been a *Devadasi*. Like many, she saw only the spiritual side."

There was silence except for the hum of the air-conditioning.

"Perhaps others understand your lives differently than you do yourself."

"Don't patronize me or you'll not get anything you wish," Kamala said sharply.

"We will continue to plan your tour and come to an arrangement, Miss Devi."

Kamala sighed. "I will communicate my conditions. For now, you must keep this Van Steen out of my sight. Now I must go. I am feeling cold. I mustn't catch a chill before the monsoon." She drew her sari across her bare shoulder.

"We will be in touch. I do understand your concerns for privacy."

She picked up the unopened bottle of whiskey. "You do not mind?"

"No, not at all, please do take it," he said.

Kamala walked to the door. "Please call my secretary, she is at my home."

10.

Kamala woke up from a dream drenched in perspiration, strands of damp hair down her neck. She wouldn't sleep until dawn now, and wouldn't be able to stop thinking about the professor. Would she really travel with chicken-neck across America? Would she have to please this unappealing man? If there were a seducer behind those glasses, she could deal with advances more easily than his insistent curiosity. At the bottom of this hovered Jules, manipulating her into making this trip and exposing more of herself.

She got up, poured water from a tumbler in the fridge, and stepped onto the verandah. Mists and rain clouds covered the sky. She paced as the surf pounded the beach. She'd get her period when the monsoon finally broke and the tension would lift, but now, she knew that sleep would not come.

When Celeste arrived, cheerful and energetic, talking about visiting a museum for the first time, Kamala spoke sharply to her.

"Must you make so much clatter? I hardly slept. Of course the bodies were naked, what do you think, that we are all as prudish as your Memsahib?"

"I am sorry, Kamala. Let me set down my parcel and make you tea."

"I suppose you have books that are making so much of a rattle, almost as if I could hear that busy brain of yours."

"I have brought you fresh pomegranate juice. The vendor said it was exceptionally sweet. I am ready to do whatever you wish."

"You know, I am a reader of novels as you are yourself, so I do not criticize you for that. Last night while I was sleepless, I began to compose a story in my head. Come over here and stop that fussing with the kettle."

Celeste sat down across a table from Kamala.

"I couldn't stop my mind from working even as I wished to sleep. I will speak aloud the story that came to me last night and you will take down the words. Just write as I say. I don't want you to interrupt with questions. When we are finished here, I will lie down again with cucumbers over my eyes, then I shall be going out."

Celestine Marie spent that night and the next day typing on Kamala's portable machine all that she had taken in dictation. At first her typing was slow because she had been used to the arrangement of letters for a French typewriter, but then she speeded up. She added connective words like "then" and "after time" so that events followed and didn't jump all over the place.

When she finally lined up pages for Kamala to read, she was already late for the Connemara and her eyes burned from looking so closely at the keys and the pages.

Kamala emerged from her bedroom stretching her arms and neck.

"You poor girl. You hardly slept. I had a good and restful nap. I am not letting you go anywhere this morning. We will call and make your excuses."

"No, I cannot do that. Mr. Charles has been calling me at the Y to request special appointments that I keep. The payment is very good. I cannot miss going."

It was evening by the time Celeste returned to the bungalow, Kamala was still there. She said she had decided to stay and read what Celeste had typed. She sipped from a gin and tonic.

"Please read from the pages you have typed so I hear aloud," Kamala said.

The True Story of Lord Ganesha's Disappearance

It is a dark night, the kind of blackness where villages seem alone in the world and stars above are grains of rice in the sky. Only a new moon's reflection on the temple tank spread a thin, uncertain crescent of light, just enough for the small band of men creeping down the village lane to find their way to the temple.

Celeste paused and asked, "Do you want to tell at what date this is occurring?"

"Yes, let us say it is 200 years in the past—1770 or thereabouts."

"How do you know all this?"

Kamala smiled. "You are not the only surprising one, Celeste. Read on."

They are six men who creep past the striped walls of the Tiruchandrum temple. They are dressed in British army uniforms and wear turbans and rags over their heads. The leader is a tall and well-built bearded Dutchman named Jan Ruytsman. His Nederlander mate, Joris Voet, is not so tall, followed by a short plump Frenchie, and a boy, very slight, with black curls, who forces the temple door open to let in the others. The remaining two wait outside. They are Indian sepoys, deserters from the British forces who have stolen uniforms for the rest of the band to disguise themselves, though all are so dirty and unshaven they look more like bandits than soldiers.

Jan and his men are suffering from hunger and fatigue after their long travel from Fort St. George, Madras, and the temple smells of incense, ghee, and marigolds disgust him. He sees with dismay that the portion of rice left each night to feed Lord Sivalingum and his elephant son, Ganesha, has already been taken away. Greedy priests, he mutters to himself, but none of this will matter soon because the object of their dangerous trek into the countryside sits there smiling before them—Lord Ganesha, his trunk curving upward, extending from his fat little body, all made of gold. The men hold torches aloft, their eyes wide, their mouths gaping at the golden god of prosperity waiting for them.

Jan first heard of the gold Ganesha from a Hebrew merchant on Coral Street in Madras. Alfonso Moses said a pure golden figurine was tucked away in a village temple in the Tanjore District. The Jew made further inquiries and located Tiruchandrum, west of the district center. The sacred treasure sat facing the black stone lingum of Lord Siva, the god of creation and destruction. Siva the Father, Ganesha the Son—the old Hebrew laughed at Hindu idolatry, worse than the Christians. Jan had always done good business with the Jews, admired their learning and scholarly ways. He himself might share a Hebrew lineage through Spanish and Portuguese Jews who fled Spain for the tolerant Netherlands.

Alfonso has sent his son Rafael, the slender boy with curls, with the Dutchmen's raiding party to guard the family share. Alfonso has promised to buy the idol. The profit will allow Jan and Joris to depart British India forever. Frenchie will head for Pondicherry, under his government's protection. The Indian foot soldiers, the sepoys, who tremble at every noise, will return to their villages with enough money in their pockets to buy their release from the British Army.

The gang has spotted Red Coats on the road but managed to elude them by keeping to orchards. The unripe fruit they've picked has played havoc on their stomachs and their spirits are low. Only the night before, Jan confided to Joris. "Two Dutchmen once backed by the power of their great nation reduced to thievery of idols in the Indian countryside, eating green mangoes and shitting on the hour, now that's ironic. The Brits will shoot if they catch us."

"We'll never give in, don't begin that gloomy talk," Joris answered from half sleep. "It's do or die; once we have our fortune, we'll leave cursed Hindustan."

"I have no argument with you there," Jan said.

"My family will stay." Rafael Moses said. "The British can't do business without Jews. They borrow up to their necks to offer jewels to their English girls or Hindu mistresses."

Jan removes a small vial from his shirt pocket and sucks laudanum into his mouth. The bitter violet tincture kills appetite, fear, and even remorse.

Now Jan and Joris look up at the object of their quest, the golden Ganesha, riding upon a black stone rat.

"The ugly rat," Joris says. "I fear he is bad luck."

"Do not worry. The rat stays here," Jan answers.

In the next moments, the sepoys and Jan truss Ganesha in a canvas sack and wind a rope to secure it. With Frenchie's help, they lower the statue carefully, then drag their bundle across the temple paving-stones as if they've committed a murder and are removing the body.

They groan under the weight until they reach a burnt paddy field. Singed dry stalks crackle so loudly that Jules whispers to Joris, "The elephants will come to rescue their own. Hurry."

"Wait, what name did you give to the Dutchman?" Kamala asked.

Celeste backed up to the sentence she just read. "I wrote what you said, Kamala. I have 'Jules' written. Oh, I see...we must change to Jan."

"Slip of the tongue." Kamala sipped her drink.

"Where did this story of Jan come from? Is this for a film script?"

"Of course, my mind thinks in terms of a movie. Carry on."

Jan follows a silver thread of moonlight in an easterly direction, aiming for the railway line between Tanjore and Trichinopoly, but sometime in the night, as they cross and recross the dry Kauvery River, he realizes he is leading his men in a circle.

Without warning, Red Coats begin shooting muskets into the orchard. The soldiers are a small force, no more than a half dozen, Jan guesses, but well armed.

"Run," Jan yells. He and Joris drag the heavy Ganesha only a few yards.

"He is too heavy," Joris says.

They are panting at the edge of a small ravine.

"Push it in, quickly. We'll come back later, now run," Jan commands.

Joris has started to run when a new round of fire from another direction erupts around them. Jan sees his mate Joris, his closest companion, veteran of cyclones, wars, whoring, and philosophizing by the light of the southern stars, take a ball in the back and fall. The next moment, a shot rips through his own shoulder and sends him tumbling down the slope into the stinking ravine, the village sewage pit, beside Ganesha.

As the sun burns his eyelids, Jan is awakened by the vile smell of excrement into which he's fallen. A few feet away, Ganesha's golden trunk seems to wave amid human waste. He can almost hear the god mocking him. Mejnherr Jan Ruytsmann, regional governor in the Celebese, possessor of wealth and beautiful women, buried in a shit hole. He vomits and lifts his head where he can see low-hanging mangoes. If only he could have a sip of that sweet juice to quench a terrible thirst, but he cannot move. Dark blood coats his arm. Pain knocks him back. The pain comes from his shoulder. He cannot move for a time, but at last he removes his vial and sips several drops of laudanum. He groans. My shipmate, my finest friend Joris—gone. Perhaps Frenchie and little Rafael Moses have escaped and will return to help me.

He knows that thirst will kill him if he doesn't find water. Thirsting to death is God's worst punishment. He uses his good hand to wipe sweat from his brow and sucks its moisture. He must find water. The night before, he saw water in the temple tank.

Each meter he crawls costs him pain beyond measure. At last he reaches the red and white striped temple wall of the Tiruchandrum temple. Once there, he lowers himself down a flight of steps like a wounded animal with only one purpose: water, no matter how green and fetid it is. Just as his tongue is about to touch moisture, he feels his head being jerked back, pulled from that saving liquor. Something as light as a bat wing brushes his face and the next moment he tastes water so fresh and cool that it cannot be from the temple tank. A girl's face hovers above him like a vision. "You mustn't drink bad water, Sir," she says.

"There should be a pause here," Kamala said. "A moment for rest. Please write that there is change of scene, the day becomes night and day again. Write that several days have passed."

"I shall make a space, as it is done in a book."

Pain forces Jan awake. He sees he is lying in a small room with cloth over windows.

"Whoever you may be, if you are no ghost and I'm still in the world of the living, bring the bottle in my pocket and give it to me, I beg you."

The temple apparition he sees now is a woman with slender arms who is keeping half of her face hidden by the end of her pale sari. A cool hand tips the vial and blessed laudanum reaches his tongue.

Jan sleeps. Daylight. Night. Day again in the small, bare room curtained against light. The vision inside his head is darker: in that withered paddy field, dogs and vultures must be feasting on Joris and the sepoys. He begins to weep. He feels a cool hand on his forehead and looks up.

The girl has one normal eye and one strange milky one. She speaks slowly, in English.

"You are hiding from British." It is not a question.

"My life is in your hands. What is your name?"

"I am called Muthu, which means Pearl. You are safe here."

He touches her cool hand and will not let go. "I shall call you Angel Pearl, for that you are to me. Or I am passed to the other side and this is a dream."

"No, Sahib, you are not dreaming."

"Then I bless you again, Pearl Angel."

He sees the girl cannot be more than sixteen and would be a young beauty except for her opalescent orb framed like a normal eye by thick black lashes. Her lips are lovely and full.

"How much remains?" He watches as she re-corks the laudanum.

"At this rate, the bottle will last three days perhaps."

"I shall make it last longer. The concoction is pure. Give me less."

Jan remembers the last evening in the Madras chemist's garden before he embarked on this disastrous affair. As they sat dreamily in an opium haze, a vision of white, an angelic vision, passed before his eyes. He saw only her profile, as if she held a mask in a drama. Like all men of the sea, he was superstitious. The vision in the garden, the girl Pearl, was his angel.

The pages Celeste had typed came to an end.

"It is exciting. I want to know what will happen next."

"You will have to wait for my next inspiration," Kamala said. "Now I'll dress and meet Hari for an evening out."

When Kamala had gone, Celeste saw there were history books lying on a table and picked up the one that had a place marked with a leather strip. *A Rendering of Accounts in the Tanjore District of Madras Presidency, 1789-1877.* The page that had been marked began with an account called "The True Story of the Theft of the Idol Ganesh from the Tanjore District."

From the first sentence, Celeste recognized the story Kamala had been relating about an idol's theft. She'd said that the setting and circumstances had come in a dream. Perhaps Kamala had been reading the book and fallen asleep. The history book had no cast of characters, no Jan in its pages, only an account of a theft and the punishment of the thieves who were caught. There was no mention of a Dutchman. Celeste admired Kamala's imagination that had created the rest.

11.

"You are our most famous Auntie the world knows!" the nephews liked to tease their aunt, Tanjore Balasaraswati. Sima, the flutist, warming up the *sol fa* scales, sat beside his brother Bamu on the long drum. Both men, in their thirties, dressed in white homespun, were both brilliant musicians who could improvise the most complex variations, whole passages on the ragas they played, but they drank too much and unlike their world-renown aunt, had done little to further their own careers. When Kamala procured work for them with the Gemini orchestras as playback musicians, too many times they had failed to show up.

Most of the guests in the backyard garden were extended family of Tanjore Balasaraswati. Aunt Gita knew the genealogy best and how everyone was related. Simu and Bamu were Kamala Kumari's second cousins. Kamala fit into the line of *bharatanatyam* dancers and their teachers on her mother's side. At the center of this family gathering reigned Balasaraswati, known as Bala, who was now in her fifties, her figure statuesque and her features softer than when she'd first mesmerized audiences with the passion and musical intelligence she expressed in every part of her supple, strong body. Her amber-colored eyes glowed with the pleasure in hospitality; the hurt she'd experienced when she was young and disrespected because of her caste seemed far in the past, but deeper down, Balasaraswati had a long memory. She didn't forget that recognition had come first from abroad, from America and England, France and Japan, and only when she began appearing at international festivals as India's greatest dancer, the high caste men of Madras began to take notice. Now, when one of the *vidwans*, the Brahmin authorities of music and dance, wanted her to preside over opening night at the Music Academy or award a prize, they had to come to her home and wait patiently for her answer.

As Bamu tuned the *mridungam,* testing pitch, tapping stones against taut leather for tone, Kamala and the old dance master Kuruvu sat side by side enjoying the fragrances of jasmine, gardenias, and roses, the vast garden lit by overhead strings of lights and lush with flowering bushes, mixing in the air with spices and juices rising from Gita's chicken curry.

Balasaraswati greeted Kamala's dance master with the respect every pupil showed a teacher. "Welcome, Master," she said, kneeling low enough to touch her head to his feet.

"I've brought you a bottle," Kamala placed Johnny Walker Black Label on the table.

"How is Grandmother?" Balaswaraswati asked.

"She is not well. Neighbors sent a telegram. I must go soon," Kamala replied.

"Then you must not wait."

"Yes, I will go to see her," Kamala answered.

Now Gita came up, took Kamala's hand and walked her to the drink table where they poured Johnny Walker into a glass, added ice.

"Kamala, my dear, how is the filming going? Does love go wrong again in this picture? Is there much weeping and travail before all ends happily?" Gita asked.

"Oh yes, much weeping. Every scene must have tears."

"How is dear Raj Tewari?" Gita and Kamala walked back toward Balasaraswati and handed her the glass.

"You wouldn't want to see him these days without his corset. His weakness is not for women but dolls and card games," Kamala said.

"And to think he's still a heartthrob! Speaking of hearts, I am being quite selfish. We have guests waiting to greet you though it seems to me one gentleman may be hiding behind plants."

Kamala knew from Gita's conspiratorial tone the identity of one surprise guest before she turned around and saw Jules Van Steen talking to Dr. Standard.

Gita whispered, "Your dear friend asked to bring an American professor. He reveres our Balasaraswati and was eager to meet her. I could not say no."

"You may know that my friend Mr. Van Steen now has a wife. An American."

"No, I did not. Oh my dear, I hope I have not made a mistake and ruined your evening. Still, you will make any wife pale with envy looking as you do tonight." Gita's eyes twinkled with mischief as she held up the fringe of Kamala's deep red sari shot with gold threads. "Go now to him and cause his heart to throb and his soul to regret."

She heard Kuruvu's voice. "I blame myself for being too soft on the girl and allowing this cinema nonsense. She should be devoting herself to dance honoring God."

"Then I wouldn't have my bungalow by the sea, would I, Guruji?" Kamala called out loudly enough for Jules to hear and know he was being put on notice. Sweeping her red sari over her shoulder, she walked toward the two men, and folded her hands before the professor.

"Good evening. You have come to the source of art." Kamala nodded toward Balasaraswati. "Thank you for the fine whiskey you have brought tonight."

"To meet Tanjore Balasaraswati in her home setting is such an honor." Dr. Standard removed his glasses and rubbed them on his sleeve. "Your friend Mr. Van Steen arranged it all. I wonder if it would offend anyone if I took some pictures. There is a flash."

"I think you should not. Let me say a word to your companion, Mr. Van Steen."

Kamala heard her own voice as if it came from somewhere outside her. Her knees felt week, a weakness that happened with Jules which she never mastered. But she was an actress who could take control and so she drew a deep breath, "Where is your wife this evening. Is she not a dancer?"

He was avoiding looking into her eyes as she was avoiding his.

"The wife you married, she is twenty years your junior? I've heard that she dances well in a western fashion! Shall I audition her? Never mind. You have lost a stone and look older, as if marriage doesn't suit."

"I understand turning up like this is irregular, but when I mentioned your family connection with Balasaraswati, my friend grew so excited I couldn't refuse his request. Gita was gracious and told me to bring him around."

"You know discretion matters to my career and you have been telling too much."

"As long as what is written is true in a general way for audiences to understand the history of the dance and caste, Dr. Standard will not violate any privacy. Names will not be mentioned."

"When I perform, this so-called true history will be written in the programs. Will they not associate me with it? I should have been consulted before you undertook revelations. From now on, I demand to see every word written and give my approval before it appears."

"I am too occupied with business to be giving it my full attention," Jules said.

"When you give it your attention, I will be informed. Good evening." She turned her back.

Sima had begun softly playing his flute. Bamu tapped the edges of the *mridungam* with his fingers. Aunt Gita moved to stand beside the musicians and followed the raga's sinuous line with her contralto. They were introducing the musical themes of a monsoon-yearning raga.

Kamala poured another inch of Johnny Walker into her glass, then stepped behind Gita and wrapped her arms around her cousin's waist and laid her chin on her shoulder.

"Show me your face, so I will not waver," Gita and Kamala sang. "Why don't you come, Krishna, my beloved, to fill this vessel with your love, soothe this heart that is burning? Are you with another lady this night?"

Though she never looked his way, Kamala sent every gesture, every movement, every glance toward Jules. She knew that the perspiration forming on her upper lip and in the curve of her breasts was a call to his desire. When she brushed her palm across her brow in longing for love, he must be remembering and suffering longing for her.

"Why don't you come, Krishna, fill this vessel with love, soothe this heart that is burning."

Kuruvu, one arm over his bald head like a stork, tapped on the garden paving, keeping time as the raga drew to its intense climax and fragrances of Gita's curry bubbling in coconut milk and chilis filled the night air.

Kamala left the musicians to fill a banana leaf with rice and curry for her teacher. Jules followed. "Let us go to talk." He held Kamala by the arm.

"There is nothing we have to be speaking of. Go home to your wife. Give my regards to the professor and please step out of my way."

A crash came from inside the house as plaster broke off the ceiling.

"That's Siva dancing destruction on our old molding. Repairs must be made before monsoon." Gita scooped extra ghee over the rice that Kamala brought to Kuruvu. "My dear," she said to Kamala, "I don't think you convinced anyone that you wish that man gone."

12.

Jules turned off the main beach onto a stretch of bumpy concrete half covered in sand. As soon as he stopped, Angela flung open the car door and ran out onto the sand. Celeste and Jules watched her take leaps toward where surf rushed up the beach.

"We have to stop her. She's barefoot," Jules said.

"And the water is so close. She is not taking care." Celeste saw surf like teeth rising from the surface of the sea, lit by the moon, then obscured by clouds.

Abruptly, Angela turned back from the water and came returning toward the car.

"Come with me, Celeste, the air makes you feel so light."

"Sand is unclean, Missy." Celeste reached toward Angela's hand to hold her.

"You should have something on your feet," Jules said.

"Oh you two, you're not fun at all."

Angela broke free and began to run back across the sand toward the line of surf.

"Missy! Don't go in the water. Go to her, Sahib, please."

"What a damn foolish girl." Jules was stripping off his trousers.

"Hurry, Sir."

"Angela! Come back! Do you see her, Celeste?" Jules ran toward the waves.

The clouds cleared again, lighting up phosphorus in the surf.

Beyond this line, she saw Angela's head bobbing between the heaving mounds of waves.

"There she is, Sahib! She's going to drown." She pointed. *Jesus and Mother Mary, save my Missy*, she began to pray.

"Why did she bolt without warning, Celeste? Has she lost her mind?"

"I don't know, Sahib. Are you not responsible for her? Are you not kind to her? Forgive me, I should not speak. Look, here she comes. Go to cover her."

Angela emerged from the waves, the surf up to her knees, and then she was out on the sand, but without her top, her trousers, without anything but her white underpants. Celeste was about to take off her own dress when Jules handed her his shirt. "Go to her," he said.

She wrapped Angela with the shirt.

"You're a foolish child, Angela. There is a bad current here," Jules said.

"It felt wonderful, as warm as milk. I had to do it, don't you understand?"

"You have no idea how dangerous it is. No one swims here. What shall we do with you?"

"We should go home and give Missy a bath and be thankful," Celeste said.

———

Celeste hesitated before opening the bedroom door the next morning, but Angela lay asleep under the netting looking peaceful and did not appear to have any ill effects from her swim. Fragrances of jasmine and orange blossoms came from a vase at her bedside. Suddaraj must have collected a bouquet. His damp shirt and Missy's dress lay waiting for Ravi to wash them.

"Amma," Ravi shook her head and sniffed the clothes. "Sahib has spell on him."

"What are you speaking of, Ravi?"

"I know a potion to help a man make his member strong and get children. I can buy in the market and we give to Sahib."

"Ravi, you know nothing, you'll say nothing. This isn't your business."

Ravi shrugged, her nose ring glittering. "Sahib called a taxi. He packed his bag and left Memsahib asleep."

Poor little bird, Celeste thought. Alone with monsoon coming. Her heart heaved as gusts of wind rattled the heavy trees and reminded her of the wild sea with her mistress in it.

Angela opened her eyes and stretched her arms over her head.

"I'm sorry I frightened you last night. I am a good swimmer. I couldn't resist."

"The sea is dangerous, Missy."

Celeste thought of the bottles of pills she'd put down the toilet and Angela's description of how impulsive she'd been.

"I have plans to discuss with you." Angela sat up and pulled a shawl over her shoulders.

"Missy, drink the tea."

"I know Jules has gone. I could leave, too, but I'm not ready to. He plucked me out of my troubles, like a dance partner who catches you just before you hit the ground, and brought me here to India. I realize I've seen so little since I've been here."

"Missy, do not talk of leaving." Celeste took Angela's hand. "I was so frightened."

"I am sorry for that and I promise I won't scare you again. Are you thinking of that big horse that ran off with the bit between his teeth?"

Celeste nodded. "And the terrible waves."

"I swam in the Indian Ocean. Those clouds, and the phosphors, it felt like being dipped in life." Angela sat up. "I knew nothing about my husband's life here so what did I expect? I've been hurt by his indifference. I thought I would matter more to him."

"You do matter. Your skin is cool, Missy. That's good, no fever."

Angela looked out the window at the sky. "It's dark already. Did I sleep through the day?"

"No, it's only noon but monsoon is coming."

"I'm here in India and the monsoon is coming. Isn't that exciting?"

"Often people die in the storms and flooding," Celeste said.

"Celeste, don't worry. What I've decided is safe. I want to learn

Indian dance. Money appears to be no problem for Jules and I can stay in the house as long as I wish."

A clap of thunder cut off Angela's words, the sound so loud breaking over them that everything rattled. Moments later, a lightning-branch turned the room phosphorescent white. Next door, college church bells clanged wildly. Celeste closed the verandah doors while Suddaraj, his khaki shorts and shirt clinging to his muscular body, ran in to shut windows.

Angela turned to Suddaraj and Celeste. "Have you heard of Kamala Kumari?"

"Why would you ask that, Missy?" Suddaraj answered suddenly.

"I want to ask her if she'll teach me dance. Remember the pictures we see all over? I think she's the most popular dancer in Madras."

"She's a cinema actress now. She won't be teaching dance," Celeste said.

"You sound as if you know her personally, Celeste."

"She was my customer at Connemara. Always busy in the movies." She turned away.

"I read in a magazine that she trained in classical dance and still teaches young girls to continue the tradition. Can you take me to her?" Angela asked Suddaraj.

"Not possible to go out, Missy." Suddaraj pointed to the storm outside.

"You can't go out on the roads now, Missy," Celeste said.

"Suddaraj, when the storm is over, I want you to take me to see Kamala Kumari."

"Storms go on for weeks," Suddaraj said.

"I don't know what it is about you two. You're so cautious."

"We only want best for you, Missy."

The lights flickered and went out. Celeste wasn't surprised. She remembered power lines down, no electricity, sitting by candlelight for their prayers.

"Let's taste this rain." Angela pushed open a window and put her head out.

13.

Jules woke to a knock on the door of his wagon-lits compartment followed by a smell of coffee. "Yes, come," he said.

"Sahib ordered coffee to start, with milk?" An India Railway servant wearing a turban and starched white jacket stood in the doorway. "You requested full breakfast."

"Thank you, both. I'm hungry." Jules reached for his dressing gown as the servant rolled in the trolley and poured black coffee from a silver thermos into a china cup, lifted a second silver thermos and poured in steaming milk. He flourished a starched napkin over the silver dome where a breakfast platter of thick bacon strips and fried eggs waited beside grilled toast drenched in butter and fruit jelly in little ceramic pots.

"Eggs prepared as you requested, Sir?" "They look perfect. Thank you." "*The Madras Mail?*"

Jules took the damp Madras newspaper. He handed the waiter a crumpled five-rupee note and settled in to read the news as he ate his breakfast.

Through the night, the train had traveled south into the monsoon, sometimes seeming to outrun the storms, other times caught in rains. Jules learned from the paper that winds had knocked down power lines and cut telephone service in southern Madras State. He might not be able to call Angela from Coimbatore. He didn't know what he would say to her, nor what she still expected after the previous night when he'd watched her, first in the tub then drying herself off.

Her body was white with a down of dark hair that he hadn't seen so much of before. It covered her delicate arms and the nape of her neck like a faint simian fur. He wondered whether she shaved when she was dancing, because his mother had shaved her arms and legs and used a chemical that smelled badly to lighten the dark hair above her mouth. When they had been in hiding and there was nothing to do, his mother complained bitterly that no one should see her because no woman should have a mustache.

Only a small step into the bathroom and he could have taken Angela in his arms to woo her for the first time. But as soon as he felt desire, he remembered the danger that Dr. Fitzgerald warned of. What if he took that step toward her and had to confess? He could not.

He backed away and went upstairs to his room on the floor above.

A shimmery morning light flooded the sky and the paddy fields alternated between being turned white in flashes of lightning and black under dark clouds. At moments, wind gusts changed the landscape as quickly as if sheets had been lifted and then lowered again over the fields. White herons rose on their tendril-like legs and flew off into darker clouds.

The train jerked to such a sudden stop that Jules was thrown against the upper bunk. When he recovered and looked out the window, he saw that workmen were trying to switch the tracks around a deep flooded area. The men's heads were wrapped in rags like the carnival roustabouts Jules remembered seeing set up tents outside Amsterdam not long after the war had ended when he and his mother had returned to the city. She took him to the circus where girls with flying black hair rode white horses bareback. Bella said they were Russian gypsies, the best riders in the world.

Once the train rolled forward again, Jules could see the outskirts of Coimbatore, and before long, they were pulling under the cover of the station. On the platform, a young man came forward, his palms together, bowing, then introducing himself as Ramu, great nephew of the Coimbatore mill owner, Dr. P. Chettiyar who Jules had come to see. Ramu wore gold rings on the fingers of both hands, and the sweet smell of his hair tonic and aftershave seemed to suck up fresh air.

"Sorry to have caused you to wait. We were stopped several times for track repair."

"No trouble. I was able to verify the train's arrival time so I would be to the minute. The Swiss are making the best watches." He showed Jules his watch. "More reliable than Indian-made."

In the car, Ramu's cologne made Jules a little nauseous. When the young man lit up a cigarette, Jules begged him not to smoke.

"Of course, Sahib. I am at your orders."

"Would you drive me directly to Uncle's building? You'll keep my bag, Ramu. When you come to collect me after I see Uncle, we'll return to the station. I won't be staying tonight."

"Mr. Jules, why do you not stay longer with the bad weather making travel unwise?"

Jules patted the man's shoulder to keep him in his seat. "We're here, thank you."

The Chettiyar building that housied Hanuman Textiles went up three stories of aqua curtain wall. At the entrance, Jules pressed the elevator button. No light came on. Power must be out. Does Dr. Paratha Chettiyar, who was in his eighties, still climb three flights of stairs? Jules wondered.

On the second floor, Jules stopped to visit the sewing rooms. At least twenty women were at their tables, their foot-treadle machines moving quickly over material although the room looked too dark for such close stitching. He stepped next door into an equally busy and orderly cutting room, floors swept, fabric lying in bright bolts. He'd never seen an Indian enterprise run so efficiently; Dr. Chetti-yar attended to the smallest details at Hanuman Textiles: there were child-care stations, western toilets with instructions spelled out in several languages, and a cafeteria in the basement that respected the dietary laws for workers of different castes.

Jules knocked on Dr. Chettiyar's door. When no one answered and it wasn't locked, he stepped into the large office. From the window overlooking the street, he saw a long blue Cadillac pull to the curb. The tips of black galoshes emerged first, followed by an umbrella, then a glow of white cotton *dhoti* and long gauzy *kurta* that Dr. Chettiyar wore so that he looked, from this distance, like Gandhi. The resemblance went further: the prominent nose and round glasses, the small stature. Indeed, Dr. Chettiyar enjoyed telling strangers on first meeting, that like the Mahatma, he had been a vain and foppish youth who only later had turned to more serious matters. Jules knew there was a major difference: during the struggle for Indian independence from the British, Dr. Chettiyar had not gone to prison nor retired to an ashram, rather he'd swallowed up cottage industries all around his district and become a wealthy man

The old man was out of breath from climbing stairs. "I am not as young as I was," he said.

"I admire your strength, Dr. Chettiyar," Jules replied.

The men made *namaste* bows to each other. Dr. Chettiyar regarded Jules by coming closer and peering at him.

"My boy, you are flourishing with marriage. I thank you for communicating this happy news. One should never remain a bachelor past twenty, very bad for health. I remember my first rapturous months of marriage. Wife is a jewel among wives to this day. Please bring your bride to meet us for *Deepavali*. Is she fair with porcelain complexion in the British way?"

"She is rather fragile, and I worry the climate doesn't suit her."

"She must visit an ayurvedic man. I shall give you names in Madras."

"Thank you. The heat affected her at first, and then she came down with Dengue fever. She is recovered and cool weather should put color in her cheeks."

Dr. Chettiyar sat behind his desk. Jules took a chair facing him. "We are having labor problems again. Agitators coming from outside, waving banners and throwing stones." He ejected a gob of red betel juice directly into a bronze pot several feet away. "Nasty habit, betel-nut chewing. I should renounce but flesh is weak."

"Alas, that is true," Jules answered.

The old man shot another well-aimed red ball into the spittoon.

"I regret that my tour of the mills will be briefer than usual, due to the season. I fear leaving my wife alone at home with monsoon beginning," Jules said.

"Of course, of course. But we do have the time for you to tell me about coming fashions for England and America and how we should proceed to be ahead of competition."

Before Jules could begin to speak, Govindum Chettiyar, the eldest grandson, knocked and entered. Govindum, square-built and dressed in a suit of striped worsted that cupped his buttocks, was the heir apparent though his grandfather gave no signs of letting go the reins. The mill owner had no sons himself, but his daughters had numerous children who, like Govindum, had been sent abroad to study business management and engineering at technical colleges in Manchester and Liverpool.

"Our polyester combinations are coming out very fine," said Govindum. "The pleats hold best I've seen. In the States, they will love convenience of no ironing."

"I'm sure they are well-made and practical, Govindum, but customers value Indian hand weave for its uniqueness. The natural, hippie style is spreading beyond the hippies."

"Mr. Van Steen, with due respect," Govindum spoke from the other side of the table, but his voice boomed, "the time when those foolish young people called hippies were influencing taste is past. More sensible sober patterns and behaviors will be coming next."

"The tastes of 1960s have influenced the 70s," said Jules. "We are only in the beginning of a changeable decade."

When they had politely argued for their point of view for some minutes, Dr. Chettiyar waved his hand for attention. "My dear nephew, our Dutch friend was recently in New York and is abreast of style. Let us continue discussing this later. I wish Mr. Jules to take a tour of the mills as rain is already coming down. It is my intention to spend these final minutes of our visit congratulating Mr. Jules on his marriage and offering gifts from the looms of Hanuman Mills. Let us have our tea."

Dr. Chettiyar rang a bell and two young men entered with their arms full. They rolled out silks on a table, a spectrum of color from turquoise to brilliant saffron. Jules picked up a heavy mauve raw silk sari shot through with gold that seemed to give off a subtle and luscious glow.

"What a beauty this is, and perfect for my wife's fair skin. Thank you," Jules bowed.

———————

They passed through the Coimbatore city center and in minutes were driving on uneven roads where tin-roofed shanties gave way to fields of rice paddy submerged by the rains. In the course of the afternoon, skirting pools of water and downed trees, Ramu escorted Jules to three Hanuman mills. At the end of his tour, Jules again insisted on being driven to the station where he discouraged Ramu from accompanying him to his train, saying he wished to visit the toilets and then purchase newspapers. He then waited until he saw Ramu drive away the station.

Jules did not go to the platform where the Express to Madras was waiting but rather crossed over on a bridge and boarded the next local train to Madurai.

The journey south and east should have taken a few hours but the train was constantly stopping at small stations or slowing through flooding on the tracks. In the light of lanterns flickering outside in the darkness, Jules saw that in places lakes of water surrounded them. Perhaps I should have gone back to Madras, he thought.

Just before three in the morning, the train pulled alongside a platform where a railway servant wearing a headscarf waved them on. Jules saw his own face in the mirror on the opposite wall. The dark circles under his eyes, heavy shadow over his jowls and chin in the chiaroscuro light shocked him: how old and dissolute he looked. He tightened his facial muscles to make disappear the double chin, but before he could look away from his reflection, he saw his mother's face emerging like an underlay of an older painting on a canvas, a Rembrandt self-portrait in which the old man was already visible in the younger man's face.

Jules closed his eyes and moved away from the mirror. He opened his flask and drank a sip of whiskey. He didn't believe in actual ghosts but rather that the dead lived inside one and could haunt memory as persistently as any spirit from another realm. Bella came to him at moments of exhaustion and doubt, her appearance in waking moments and dream not malignant like that of his father, rather as longing for her touch and the rich smell of her, which shamed him.

"Your job, little man, is to take care of women in need," she'd directed him when, indeed, he was her 'little man.' He remembered how jealous his father had been of him over Bella's attention. She wanted little Jules and not Henryk to sponge her white shoulders, her white neck with fine dark hairs at the nape. When Bella lifted herself from the tub to give him her back to rub, her breasts, large, pink and buoyant, floated last from the water.

Bella took him to the theater where the chorus girls made a fuss over the handsome boy, but he wouldn't kiss anyone but his mother. The girls teased him, "You love your mama more than all others in the world." It was true, he loved his mother so much.

He remembered how Bella dabbed the last drop of *L'Heure du Temps* on her neck for the appointment at Gestapo headquarters. "Don't you worry, darling, I will be home soon," she said.

When she returned, Jules didn't smell the carnation perfume, only an odor of sweat and fear. The Germans kept her passport.

"They'll be back. They can smell a Jew." Henryk told her.

"I'm a Dutchman's wife," Bella protested, holding Jules' hand.

"You must pack yourselves tonight," Henryk had insisted.

Despite the deprivation in space and nourishment, Bella practiced her dance positions every day in the windmill where they lived for nearly a year, the last of it on tulip bulbs.

Jules' thin arm was her barre for *pliés, tendus, battus.*

"A dancer must never give up doing her exercises or she'll lose her physique. Madame Pavlova had a way of rehearsing us that was unique. She made us visualize how movements would look from the audience. Some stages were so small that we girls crowded together and the wings on our *Sylphides'* costumes scraped. The English girls were jealous of me because I was prettier and could speak Russian and Polish with Madame. British girls lacked the Slavic temperament, Madame told me."

Bella said Pavlova was a great flirt, a coquette surrounded by homosexuals. "Madame once declared sex was like medicine. You should not like it but only take some because it did you good. I admired her dedication to her art, but I was a passionate girl who loved men."

The last months in the windmill, Bella grew weak and sometimes fell into a half-sleep where Pavlova seemed to come to her as an angel. She moved her thin arms following the notes of an interior Chopin nocturne as if she were dancing *Les Sylphides* alongside her idol.

Once when she opened her eyes, she remembered Anna Pavlova's premonition of her death as if the ballerina and the company had come to her in a dream.

"We were completing our French tour in Cannes on New Year's Eve, all of us were enjoying our champagne and as gay as could be when a pigeon flew in an open window and landed on Madame's shoulder. She left the party immediately. We learned that instead of returning to her room to sleep, she went to the cemetery to visit the grave of her first love. You see, Russians believe when a bird flies indoors it is an omen of death, and this bird had chosen her. The following evening on our way to Paris there was a derailment. No one was hurt. Madame suddenly became happy again. She told us she believed the accident was the bad luck that the pigeon signaled, but that it had passed.

We continued to Paris in a good mood, drinking champagne. We didn't know Madame had taken a chill in the graveyard. She seemed normal in Paris, but in The Hague she could not leave her bed. She died in the *Hotel des Indes*, the Hotel of India. An astrologer in Madras had predicted she'd die in India and return there in another life."

Jules believed that if the war had gone on a month longer, Bella would have died and he would have been left alone with her body. Even now, the fear of that happening, chilled him.

"Watch the sky," Henryk had written on a scrap of paper. "Be brave, my dears."

First came the planes flying over, dropping food packages. The American soldiers who carried them from the windmill arrived in a truck. They stopped many times for the families of Jews and Gypsies who'd survived by hiding in towers like their own. They also came out of the strangest places that Jules had ever seen, from tunnels leading to the sea, at the mercy of the tides.

After the war, Henryk installed his wife and son in a small apartment in Amsterdam while their old rooms were repaired. Henryk was seldom at home; bit by bit, Bella and Jules learned that during the war, Henryk had been a double agent, an agent in the Dutch Underground at the same time that he had collaborated as a food distributor for the Occupation. The Germans trusted Henryk to provision their troops, and to obtain cheese and bread the Dutch were denied. When the Underground derailed the shipments Henryk had alerted them to, the Germans never suspected their trusted supplier. At victory ceremonies, Henryk received decorations as a hero of the Underground; but his talent as a consummate con man didn't end with the war. Henryk cheated American soldiers who entrusted him with dollars to change into guilders. When three soldiers came asking for their money, they only found a woman and child at home. One soldier made Bella sit down.

"Your husband is a cheat. That's bad enough but do you know he's also an opium addict? He'll never be able to take care of you."

A month later, Henryk van Steen was found dead in a whore house in The Hague. Wartime friends came to console the widow. None could understand how a decorated fighter for the Resistance could die with a needle in his arm. The death got hushed up and Bella received a pension due a war hero.

She took back her stage name, Bella Rosa, and opened a dancing school in their old apartment with high ceilings, dark drapes and heavy furniture. She had a brief stage comeback in 1960, long after Jules had left home. Past fifty, overweight, with bad teeth, the Nederlands Ballet hired Bella as a character dancer; onstage again, she surprised everyone with her aplomb. Reviewers wrote praise in newspapers she sent to Jules at his ports of call. "Dressed in maroon velvet and a cape trimmed with ermine, Bella Rosa's round arms and dark eyes evoke moody dances of Hungary and Warsaw."

After barely a half year of her come back, the stage manager had wired Jules that his mother had tripped on a rug and fallen in her dressing room. She'd hit her head on her makeup table and never woke up. A month later, with the obituary, the ballet manager sent the Indian jewel box that Anna Pavlova had given his mother when she was a young girl.

14.

Jules walked into the main hall in the Madurai train station where hundreds of passengers were waiting out the monsoon that had left them stranded. At one end of the hall he saw a space and made his way as courteously as possible through the dense crowd. He squeezed in next to a small man sitting cross-legged on the bench. The man had white hair to his bare shoulders over which he draped a shawl, and a *dhoti* tied between his thin legs.

Jules sat for what seemed a very long time trying not to disturb the man's meditation. Finally, unable to sit any longer, Jules pointed to his black travel bag and across the hall where a line of men must be waiting for bathrooms. Jules apologized for interrupting him.

"Would you watch this for me?" Jules asked.

"No worry." The man smiled briefly at Jules and shut his eyes again.

He reached the entrance but from a few feet away, the stench repulsed him. He couldn't go in there. He'd have to find somewhere else, a restaurant or hotel with a lavatory that would be less repulsive than this one.

He returned to pick up his bag and thanked the man who still had his eyes closed. Jules felt curious about a person who seemed to keep himself separate from the noise and smells. He would have liked asking how he reached such composure.

Outside the station, Jules breathed deeply the moist air with a moment of relief before a burst of thunder and then a downpour of rain so intense and powerful, as if a bucket of cold water had been overturned directly on him, forced him to run. Below, women had hiked up saris to their knees and men tied their *dhotis* at their waists to wade down the flooded lower steps. He rolled his trousers and ducked his head into his jacket as he hurried with the crowd toward the shelter of the Meenakshi Madurai temple that glowed even in rain with its Technicolor pinks and greens.

Inside the temple was as dark as the exterior was bright, the heavy air pungent with jasmine, ghee and sweat. When his eyes got used to the darkness, Jules saw figures kneeling, face down on the dank stones chanting their prayers. People were pressed so closely together that only at the last moment did he feel the strong arm grasp his shoulder, the elbow lock around his neck as a hand pulled at his travel bag. The arms dragging him backward were about to get away with his bag when a voice shouted, "Thief, thief." He felt a shift in the weight behind him, jerked free, bag still in his hand.

Jules caught his breath and bent over double for a moment. He checked his pocket where he felt his billfold.

"Sir, are you quite all right?" a voice asked. Barely visible, he recognized the older man with long hair from the station. He was shorter than Jules had thought, barely up to his shoulder.

"Very bad men taking advantage," the man said.

"You saved me. Thank you."

"I did nothing to return their violence," the man said.

"Whatever you did, thank you. But can you tell where there is a WC? I need it badly."

"Sir, I know a place nearby. We will find all we require there."

The man took his arm and they made their way through the temple crowds and back out onto the street.

"Sivaram Rao." The man bowed, hands together.

Jules returned his *namaste* and introduced himself. "Thank you again."

Rao led him to a tea shop where a girl in a black sari directed Jules to the back of the room. The hole in hard dirt was malodorous but welcome. There was water to wash his hands and face.

Rao had ordered cups of milky tea and biscuits for them.

"Thank you again, something sweet is what I need. I feel chilled.

But you, Mr. Rao, you're dressed so lightly. Aren't you cold?"

"We do our own weaving and the cotton is quite resistant to weather."

"Weaving? Tell me about your enterprise and perhaps I can help you sell goods."

"I do not know if enterprise is the word. We are a spinning cooperative in a village near Madurai. We support ourselves and live quietly. I came for shopping before the monsoon but was forced to shelter myself last night in the station. I should return home with supplies before night falls." Rao looked upward. "But if the skies do not agree, so be it. What will be, will be. Trains may not be running."

"I'm fortunate that squall sent you to my side. I wouldn't have a rupee or my belongings if you hadn't scared off the men from robbing me."

"I wouldn't have hit them, but shouting, perhaps shouting in the circumstances, was necessary. In our community, we practice non-violence, following Gandhi."

"Tell me about your cooperative work." Jules sipped the sugary tea.

"We spin and card cotton that we weave into handcrafts such as place mats and napkins to sell at the government emporiums."

"I purchase weaving from cooperatives and supply them to markets abroad who appreciate the handiwork. I was just in Coimbatoire to visit Chettiyar mills."

"Sri Hanuman Chettiyar? They are big enterprises, perhaps more to your needs but I am sorry not to have examples of our labor with me."

"I know Chettiyar was a profiteer during your country's struggle for independence but he now repents that, or so he says. We have done business a long time but I also like to support smaller producers, so perhaps you'll send samples to me in Madras, or I could visit." Jules handed Rao his card. "Let's have something more than tea and cake. I'm very hungry, are you?"

Rao asked the waitress to bring them *samosas* and *dhal.* "Is that to your liking, Sir?"

"Yes, but no more formality, please lease call me Jules. I have put myself in your hands twice now."

"Thank you. Jules, so please tell me, you are coming from what country? Not British?"

"Holland is my native land, but I have adopted India as my home."

"You are from the country of tolerance. I know the writings of Erasmus and of Spinoza. Enlightened minds, beautiful thinkers."

"I find it surprising to meet a man so learned. I don't mean that as it might sound but I never have read the books you name."

"In my youth, I was something of a rebel, resisting a caste marriage, belonging to the radical wing of the Congress party, serving one year in British prison for it. In confinement, I read everything passed to me and came to the conclusion that *satyagraha*, our nonviolent struggle for self-determination, would free us from British rule and unite us as a nation. In the first instance, I was correct, we have our freedom. Alas, Gandhiji's dreams have not been realized as respects the caste system that persists. Caste prejudice is a stain on our country."

"My childhood was under the German occupation. My mother was Jewish. We were in hiding until the war ended. I share your dislike for prejudice."

"Gandhiji said he would have carried arms against that great European evil."

"My father did dangerous things against the Germans but after the war, he turned out to be unreliable. I've been thinking how that time in hiding and the fear we felt continually are still with me, not that I fully understand the effects."

"I have always admired the Hebrews, the people of the book. Are you by any chance a person who is also writing a book?"

"I have my subject and a great need to write about it, but I lack discipline."

"Please give me a preview of your themes. Perhaps speaking will be of help."

"Do you really wish to hear my unfinished project? You may find it repugnant though it does concern Hindu caste so perhaps you will enlighten me where I am going wrong."

Rao drew his palms together, lowered his head, and smiled. "The Hinduism of Gandhi, like the Christianity of Tolstoy or Judaism of your Spinoza, was true to the highest spirit. Then came the fear of freedom and the laws and rules to keep us in line."

"What interests me is a particular instance of the caste system that reduced an entire group and all their descendents into a kind of slavery."

"Are you speaking of the Harijan or Untouchable caste?"

"Untouchables of the most unlikely kind, artists, dancers, singers. I believe that the *Devadasi* caste in South India originally were spiritual seekers so swept away by their devotion to Krishna that they left their homes and families."

"Perhaps the young people who come to India and give up their comforts are like this?"

"That's true, Rao. But these women had nowhere to return to. They were kept low by the stigma of promiscuity which they had been forced into by the Brahmins who exploited them."

"Please continue. I am becoming excited." Rao's faced had become flushed.

"These women, when they were young and beautiful, were also considered sacred vessels serving deities in the temple, was that not true?" Rao nodded. "What haunts me is that there's no written history to help answer the question of how these girls became women of such impurity they cannot be touched or married in the usual way. The injustice and harm obsesses me. I seek answers from women I believe are members of this caste." Jules looked away from Rao's inquiring eyes. "Here is where I myself fall into disgrace."

Jules' hands had started shaking. Rao reached across the table to calm him.

"Are you suffering from delayed shock after the attack on your person?"

"No, I'm not. I am afraid and ashamed of my own involvement with the women I have intended to help but have exploited out of weakness, some kind of compulsion I can't resist."

"What do you wish to do for these poor creatures?'

"I do not know, Mr. Rao. Redeem them in some way. But I do the opposite, I use them."

"I advise patience, my dear fellow. Understanding will come and actions will follow."

"Thank you. I feel peaceful being with you. Perhaps I haven't been able to express, that is confess myself, until now."

"Let me ask, if it is not too impertinent, what would you say are your personal weaknesses that make you feel so vulnerable at this time?"

Rao's question took Jules by surprise, but he didn't feel threatened by it. Rao sat opposite, with rain pouring down on the café's roof, like a figure of compassion, a man who did not judge.

"My relations with women are unhealthy and harmful though I wish no harm," he said.

Rao looked at Jules' gold wedding band. "Is there a person involved who is not your wife?"

"I'm a dishonest husband. The truth is, I have no intimacy with my wife. I can tell myself there are honest reasons for this but I know my behavior is not honest, not normal. My doctor says I am a walking disaster. I've kept a dear girl in the dark about it."

"What do you mean?"

"I've contracted sexual infections. I can be cured of course, but that's not the whole story." Jules paused. "I conceal from my wife my attachment to another woman who caused me such grief that I broke with her, but I'm not free of her."

"Such intense emotions. I envy you them, your nature of fire and passion."

"On the train coming here, I was thinking of my mother as I often do. I'm not free of her either. If I were in Europe, I'd consult a psychoanalyst."

Rao spoke so softly Jules leaned forward to hear "You mean the talking cure?"

"That's what it's called. There may be doctors here but I'd probably not go to them. I have a long habit of concealment. Like my father, I realize. Oh my god." Jules buried his face in his hands.

"You are talking freely to me without concealment. To be open to you in return, I have no feelings toward my wife. I am cold to her. Only cinema actresses excite me. I was going to indulge myself this afternoon with two hours of pleasure at the movies, strictly against our ashram rules."

"I am sorry to have taken your time from that pleasure."

"Oh, no. This conversation is more healthy." Rao's dark eyes glistened almost as though he were crying. "Do you personally know any actresses?"

"The woman who has bewitched me is a cine starlet with ambitions to stardom."

"Will you reveal the person's name?"

"Kamala Kumari."

"Kamala Kumari! I am crazy about the woman. I have only seen two films but she tantalized me. You must enlighten me, Sir."

"In the early days of our relationship we were truly in love and wanted nothing but to be with each other. I ceased my wandering. She filled my every moment and I could barely endure being away from her. Into this happiness came jealousy. No matter how many times she said she loved me, an admiring look from a stranger made me lose my mind and become a person she hated, even feared."

Before they could say more, thunder crashed outside.

"I've asked too much. Forgive me. I must go to the station." Rao rose. "Heavens speak."

Jules stood and held Rao's arm. "Must you go? It's my fault for burdening you."

"I asked but perhaps I did not want to hear how a man and woman can love," Rao said.

"You have become my trusted confidant, all in the course of a few hours. I'm afraid we may never see each other," Jules said.

"We will not lose touch, be assured of that. We have met for a purpose."

15.

Celeste's favorite month of the year had always been January when the *Soeurs* brought out cardigan sweaters from the cedar chests in the storeroom, sweaters that smelled of camphor with tags in the back from Le Samaritaine and Galeries Lafayettes. Whenever she put her lavender cardigan over her shoulders, she felt as if she were wearing a bit of Paris. As it did in Pondicherry, the air stayed cool for almost two months after the monsoon in Madras, and during this short time between rains and March when temperatures rose, she had learned to ride a bicycle. Suddaraj had loaned her his cycle before Angela bought two used ladies bikes so they didn't have to rely on a car or bus to go the Music Academy. Celeste practiced up and down the long drive next door to the Women's Christian College until she felt she wouldn't wobble when Angela took her past College Road into traffic.

The first time she cycled alone onto Mount Road without Angela, Celeste was gripping the handle bars so tightly she almost tipped herself over. She waited until there was a break in traffic to enter the flow of vehicles going around Gemini Circle. She tried not to be too nervous with the din of lorries, buses, motorbikes and rickshaws, but the noise seemed as fierce as the ocean. Above her, the photograph of Kamala Kumari smiled down advertising the opening of *Pirates of the Coromandel.*

At the first exit from the Gemini roundabout, she took the smaller road to the lane where Salomé told her she lived. They hadn't seen each other during the rains. Salomé reproached her for not keeping in touch though Celeste didn't think the accusation fair: she hadn't

known where to find her friend since Salomé had quit the Connemara Beauty Salon not long after she herself had told Mr. Charles
she wasn't coming back. Salomé had also left her room at the YWCA.

When Celeste arrived at the block of new flats, Salomé was waiting outside, wearing an aqua blue silk *shalwar kamize,* a white and
gold scarf over her shoulders and dangling gold earrings. Perhaps it
was the eye make up she wore or the high heeled shoes that made
her school friend look older, no longer a girl but a woman. Celeste
wondered how her friend paid for an apartment if she had left her
employment. Perhaps she had found a better salon.

"You are perspiring. Don't sit on my new sofa. Come here into
the kitchen where I have plastic chairs. Why didn't you take a taxi?
Riding a bicycle is unladylike."

"But I don't have to wait for anyone to take me. How are you,
Salomé? You look so smart. Is this your apartment all to yourself?
How many rooms are there?"

Salomé smiled. "Come, I'll fix coffee. You will see the kitchen."

She saw a spotless refrigerator and stove. A breeze blew white curtains.

"I have only begun to decorate and complete furnishings." Salomé
brought a copper inlaid tray with a coffee pot and a plate of sugar cookies. "I know how you like your sweets. You have to watch your waistline.
Soon I will be watching mine." Salomé patted her mid-section.

"The cookies are very good. Will you be eating chocolates and
kulfi all the time?"

"You still don't understand because you're such a girl. Even though
I have given you opportunities, you haven't really benefitted as I
have." Salomé moved gold bangles up and down on her arm. "You
do not approve."

"I am grateful to you for the opportunities. Why would I not approve?"

"Because I am with Kapoor in this flat. We are living in sin."

"Oh." Celeste was silenced by her friend's words.

Salomé tossed bangs from her forehead. "Is this not a first-class
apartment? You say nothing. You disapprove of course? You will write
the *Soeurs* about me?"

"Of course I'll only write what you wish. If you are happy and have security, I am not judging you. Who is this friend Kapoor?"

"He was my client at the Connemara. Perhaps you never noticed because you had the stars coming to you. I am glad no longer to be on my feet all day, especially now. You had all the glamour patrons, though you are still not as fashionable as you could be. Will I be seeing your picture in *Cine Stars* at a party?"

"No, you will not, and the two people who employ me are more difficult than you think."

"Kapoor works for Bank of India. He will move to a senior position before long."

"Is he older than we are?"

"Of course, did you think he's a boy, how foolish you are. Do you see that I am changed?"

"You look very like a woman. I thought that when I saw you just now, that only some months back we were both girls with pigtails in the *Couvent*."

Celeste glanced at the time on the new watch with the white wrist band that she had bought for herself and liked seeing on her arm. Salomé cleared her throat.

"If you did not realize it, I am going to become a mother."

Celeste looked at her watch again as if it might help her find the right words. "Salomé Thomas! I did not know you had married. Your husband is happy with the news?"

"Yes, he is proud. He lives with his family and comes several times in the week because he is happy only with me. We are going to Bombay on holiday next month before I look fat."

"He lives with parents?"

Salomé sighed. "Little one. How can I say this to one so innocent. Kapoor has a wife, not of his choosing. I am the woman he has fallen in love with. Look at you blushing."

"Oh Salomé. I am shocked, I do admit that you are going beyond what I understand. I will have to adjust to the news."

"What shocks you the most? Have you never seen a man and a woman in love? Have you only read about love in books?"

Celeste shook her head. "We are only eighteen."

"You will be a young godmother, if you don't condemn me. I shall have the baby baptized even though Kapoor is Hindu. You will be at my side, won't you?"

"Of course I will, Salomé." She felt tears come to her eyes, then pour out, and she let herself cry loudly and without control.

"Why are you crying?"

"Because…you will be in danger. What if…"

"If you think I am not prudent, don't worry. I keep my own bank account, and I save each month from the housekeeping money Kapoor provides. He gives me many presents as well, so do not imagine that I will go back to the *Couvent* with a baby I cannot keep. Now, please, don't cry, I beg you, let us both be happy. A baby, imagine that, my baby. I'll be a good mother."

"I don't know what to think."

"I was angry for years at a mother who knew me enough to love and keep me but did not do so. I was two years when I came to the *Couvent*. I remember her, like you remember your Thérèse. I tried praying that I was not cursed, or ugly, and that was not the reason she left me, but once I decided to improve my life, I began to understand better that my mother must have been in difficulty and that she believed the *Soeurs* would raise me better than she could. Now I forgive her. Perhaps I will try to find her if that's possible. Do you forgive your mother?"

"Yes, I do. I believe she had no choice in whatever happened before I was born."

"But not that fairy story, you don't believe that?" Salomé asked.

Celeste dried her eyes and ate a cookie. "Tell me about the man you love."

"As I said, he's not as young as we are. He liked me at first meeting. He says I am a princess. He's fair and handsome. I had to hide my crush from Mr. Charles who was jealous. That ugly man imagined I cared for him. He repelled me. Once I told Kapoor, he took me from there, and forbid me from returning to work. You see what a man he is. I hope that we will have a girl with his height and my green eyes. We will prepare our daughter for the cinema."

"You should send her to college which is much better, especially if one is not fair-skinned."

"Forgive me, we have known each other all our lives and I don't think of you as dark skinned. You are so lively and pretty and always the favorite with the *Soeurs*."

"They saw your beauty and how you must be careful."

"La Mère punished me for vanity. How could I help looking as I do?"

"As I could not help it that I was not fair-skinned?"

"Yes, that is true, but look at you now, even if you're a little plump-ish as you are, with a Memsahib and a film actress. Pretty frocks, driven in American cars. But yes, of course, we will send our child to a private college, even though I am not so fond of reading as you. Kapoor is going to purchase a television, so there will be movies to see at home in comfort." She touched her stomach. "There will be a time when I will not go out and show myself. Will you still be my friend and visit? We can watch the programs on television together."

"I've only heard of television but not seen one. Of course I will be your friend as I have been, but now I must be leaving." Celeste looked at her watch, knowing she was late. She shouldn't have stayed so long but now she felt disloyal leaving her friend.

"Are you going now for business for that film star? Do they all call you Celeste?"

"Yes, everyone does. You remember I also have been a helper for the Dutch Sahib's wife. She is now studying the dance here."

"I don't like being alone all the time. You will come again soon?"

"Of course I will."

———

As Celeste cycled toward Mylapore to join Angela before her dance lesson ended, she felt only relief at leaving Salomé, but as the wheels of her bicycle turned over the pavement, a feeling of sadness replaced relief. She wished her life and that of her friend could be as simple as it had been with the *Soeurs*. Horns honked and she shook off thoughts to be careful on the road as she wheeled again around Gemini Circle toward the Music Academy. Now, with the sun bright overhead, the cardigan sweater she had worn felt scratchy and hot.

The class was almost over when Celeste arrived. Ankle bells were jingling with rapid steps. She took a seat along the wall and watched as Angela followed the three little girls standing closest to Kamala Kumari. They danced quick as wind-up toys, all brown thin arms and legs, while Angela's white arms moved more slowly.

"So, let us start again. *Sa sa, sa ma ga ma*," Kamala sang.

After one more exercise, Kamala Kumari bent her knees, raised her arms over her head, palms pressed together. Angela and the girls bowed back.

Angela sat on the floor, stretching her legs, her head to her knees.

"May I ask, why are your feet deformed?" Kamala was staring at Angela's toes.

Celeste winced but the question didn't seem to offend Angela.

"Most ballet dancers have awful feet because of our shoes that have wood in the toes so we can put all our weight on them. But we always get blisters and bunions, and often we injure ourselves, all so that we can look as we're floating in the air. Being able to dance barefoot was what I loved about modern, and here, you keep your feet on the ground. It's so connected to earth."

"Feet are important to Hindu men. You must apply oil to your toes so your husband will find you more beautiful."

Kamala sent a sideways look at Celeste who felt trapped on all sides. Salomé, now Kamala Kumari and her Missy, all people she hid truths from. Then Kamala picked up her bag and said, "Let us visit my cousin and old friend, Pattu. Today she is celebrating her daughter's engagement to a very handsome boy. She is doing a *pongol* rice ceremony. It is a happy event."

The woman who opened the door had a beautiful round face, plump arms and honey-colored skin; she smelled of sandalwood oil and roses. She was wearing more gold rings, wrist bangles and necklaces than Celeste had ever seen.

"Pattu Chettiyar, my friend, my sister, you look very well. This is a blessed day." Kamala bowed over her folded hands.

The honey-skinned woman bowed in return. "I am honored you visit on this auspicious day. Come."

They climbed a flight of stairs into a hall where three large white refrigerators stood like sentinels against the walls. "The latest model my husband is selling. He won't allow food on the shelves, but there is ice. I have foreign whiskies, gin and brandies, Kamala. May I offer you young ladies lemon squash?"

"I will have gin. Squash for my student, Angela, from America, and my helper, Celeste," Kamala said.

"Cook has prepared sweet rice to celebrate the betrothal. And here is my fortunate girl, my daughter, Mira, who will soon be a bride."

A young woman slowly rose from where she'd been lying with a magazine on a couch. She was taller than her mother, very slim, with the same honey-toned skin.

Mira showed Kamala her wedding collar of pearls and gold with earrings and rings to match. "Papa has bought this dowry though my fiancé is a modern boy, Auntie Kamala."

"I know the handsome boy. He is my friend Raj Tewari's nephew."

"Do you suppose that I will become a star like you?" Mira gave a toss of her hair.

"No you won't, my girl. Your father will not permit dancing in films or any other kind of performance. Mira, you will be a respectable wife as I am." Pattu spoke fiercely.

"Then we must hurry to see you dance before he returns," Kamala said.

Pattu shook her head. "I cannot go against husband's wishes. He forbids dance."

"My friend Pattu had many admirers for her artistry. Her husband was the fortunate favorite and won her hand."

"Oh, I wish you'd dance, just for us. I would love to see you," Angela said.

"You must indulge my student, Pattu, At least one *padam*, one song."

"Papa won't return until this evening, so indulge us, Mama," the daughter said.

"One *padam* with you, because I cannot refuse a guest," Pattu said.

Kamala walked to the center of the room, pulled up her sari, tied the pleats around her waist. Pattu stood beside her and began to sing in a low contralto.

"She is saying, 'On the boat of truth, the boatman was my true guru. I came across the sea of existence to find him.'" Kamala translated and then blended her voice with Pattu's. "I will tie on the ankle bells of love, I will wear the dancing garment before Him. Worldly modesty, family honor—I will not care for either. I will go and lie in the bed of my beloved. I, Meera, will dye myself in Krishna's blue color."

"Oh, that's beautiful! To dye oneself the color of love, how beautiful!" Angela exclaimed.

"You see what we feel in our hearts for Krishna," Kamala said. "Pattu cannot stand still."

Pattu's footwork was not so precise as Kamala's, but she moved her weight gracefully, and when she sang, her voice had such a soft tender appeal that Celeste closed her eyes, remembering one lovely girl at the *Couvent* with such a voice. Alas, the girl had been caught in the rains, developed a chill and died of fever when she was only twelve.

"I love Krishna so much," Pattu said when she stopped singing.

"As I do," Kamala answered and sat down with her drink.

A boy entered to serve them the *pongal* rice that Celeste thought delicious. Sweet tasting food was always a relief when her mind was troubled. The soft rice, perfumed with almonds and rose water, was like a kind of *kulfi* ice cream without being cold. She accepted a second helping and Pattu heaped her plate.

"How is your special friend, the tall handsome fellow?" Pattu asked.

The mouthful of rice stuck in Celeste's throat.

"Hari is well, thank you. He arranges for his car to take me where I wish to go."

———

Dusk was falling as they left Pattu's and drove through Thousand Lights.

Small boys in white skullcaps cycled by in shirts as airy as moth wings, while the Mohammedan women in their black cover-ups walked along the edge of the road. The air smelled sooty from the mutton kabobs cooking on charcoal burners. Celeste realized how little she had known about Salomé those early days in Madras when they'd come here.

"Is there anything the European husband denies his wife?" Kamala, seated up front by the driver, turned to ask Angela. "He allows you to go about at all hours. Does he know where you are now? You could be meeting with a lover and he wouldn't know."

"He knows I'm crazy about learning dance," Angela said.

"Does your husband trust you with me? Perhaps I'm a bad influence."

"How can giving me a joy like this be a bad influence? I'm healthy. I've told him how being a student of yours makes me feel back to myself. Why would he not trust you?"

Celeste felt the silence before the next words thrum in her head.

"Before I came to India, he talked about you," Angela said

Kamala turned around and looked back over the front seat. "Oh, really! Did he now? May I ask you what he said?"

"That you were the best dancer of your generation trained with great tradition but that you were an actress in the movies here, and that it was unfortunate because there were so many women in movies but none who had your heritage of dance."

"As though he knew! Well, it doesn't matter because I am on my way in the cinema whatever ignorance he has on the matter. May I ask another question, woman to woman?"

"You are my teacher and I am your pupil who must obey."

"When you go to the British clubs or to a dinner party, does your husband keep a keen eye on you to prevent flirtations with other men?"

"We haven't been at that Club for months. I only ate there once. Dull, unfriendly. Ask Celeste about those British women and how they treated us."

"Missy, you must tell."

"Well, they disrespected Celeste and Suddaraj in a way I've never seen people treated. They are the least likable women I've ever met, stupid and prejudiced. I realize I'm not familiar with British customs, but I saw enough to not to want to cross paths with those women again."

"Is this strong view unusual for an American?" Kamala asked.

"I don't know about other Americans except that officially we don't approve of prejudice. I now have a chance to be with you, my teacher. Why would I want to waste time with anyone else?"

"So you give your husband no worries?"

"If any man saw me when you were present, they would not give me a second look."

Celeste let out her breath. Angela had spoken the magic words.

"It is true, I have many admirers," Kamala said.

"Shall we get down here, Missy, to walk a while in the warm air? We'll go for *kulfi* in my favorite shop."

"After *pongal* rice! Celeste, you will be as fat as Pattu before long." Kamala reached around from the front seat and took Angela's hand. "You are pleasing to me."

"You are too kind to me," Angela replied.

"Be careful in the dark with strange men about."

When they were alone and the car had driven away, Angela said. "She is wonderful but rather insecure for someone so famous. Why do think this is, Celeste?"

16.

Celeste left for early Mass at St Thomas Mount before anyone could reach her by telephone at the YWCA. She sat at the back of the cathedral where the whiteness of the arches and the light filtering through the stained glass windows returned her to the secure feelings she had with the *Soeurs*. She knew the liturgy and responded with the worshippers to the priest's call for prayers. After the service, she knelt in her place as other worshippers lined up on the outside aisle to confess. How difficult would it be to express the confusion she felt? And what were her sins? Concealment certainly, but if she weren't ready to confess to Angela, what would telling her story to a priest do? Still, as she walked out into the blazing sun, she felt the comfort of the Mass.

From the YWCA to St Thomas Cathedral was too far to cycle so she'd ridden several buses. There were few other travelers this morning as she headed back to Adyar and Kamala's bungalow, and the chatter around her sounded cheerful. She was still weighing in her mind the reasons for revealing to Angela what she knew about Kamala Kumari's involvement with the Sahib versus keeping quiet as her Missy continued in strength and good health from taking the dance lessons. And what did she actually know as a fact about Kamala Kumari and Jules except that they no longer were friends? She told herself she was doing more good than harm keeping separate paths for everyone to follow and hoping they would not cross.

"Adyar, Beach Road" the bus driver called out. Celeste would have liked sitting longer, even venturing to look more closely at the sea but she pulled the cord and the bus stopped.

Kamala Kumari barely gave her a moment to catch her breath. "I have everything in my head. I don't want to lose a thought so let us begin."

Kamala lay on her couch fanning herself with pages that appeared to be notes. Before she began to read, she looked up, and as if in answer to an unasked question about Madras history, said, "This section is not entirely original, but film plots and songs as well as all children's tales come from Rama and Krishna, who come from our epics, so tell me what is original in India? There is no beginning nor end to our stories. It is all in the use one makes of character and the emotions."

The Girl with the Pure Heart Continued

Pearl sits on the edge of the charpoy fanning the wounded Sahib with her palm leaf. Sometimes his face twists and his eyes roll in their sockets, and Pearl is afraid he is possessed by naginis, the ghosts of abandoned and murdered girls that keep to the walls and slither out as serpent-women haunting the temple waters and river banks to seek their revenge.

Pearl and Auntie have two rooms. She has pushed the charpoy into the back room away from the lane so that villagers wouldn't see in. Not a breath of air moves. Pearl's auntie is away for a week or a month, the old woman never tells Pearl her plans, keeping them as secret as the names of female patients whose babies she delivers and those who will not be born into this lifetime. "I help them avoid their karma," Auntie says. She is an auspicious guest at weddings because she was a Dasi, married to God and thus will never become a widow. Auntie has a treasure box with Star Pagodas and rupees she believes she has hidden from Pearl in the mango orchard, but the girl knows just where it lies. Pearl has often thought of taking the Star Pagodas and running away to the city, perhaps to find work in one of the British hospitals because she knows nursing, but as great as her wish to leave is the fear of being mocked by strangers for her milk-eye. And the sounds of her village waking up, the scrabbling of chickens to find a grain or grub before sunrise, the wooden wheels in the lanes bringing dung back from the fields, are all she has known.

She is afraid that the wounded man's violet tincture is running out, and because she has seen consequences of sudden opium withdrawal in soldiers she's nursed, she knows that deprivation can cause their intestines to collapse and their brains to overheat. A man can become like a rabid animal. She dreads that moment when the Sahib's cursing and shouting will betray him. She grinds valerian root with Auntie's ayurvedic powders to calm nerves and induce more sleep.

When the Sahib regains consciousness, she is reassured that he is in his right mind. He asks her name again. "In Tamil and Telegu, I am called Muthu. In your language, my name is Pearl. I did not understand what you were saying when you were dreaming and calling out."

"I am Jan, I am a Nederlander, not English. How long have I lain here? What did I say?"

"You have been here for three days."

"I owe my life to you, my angel," he tells her.

"You talked in sleep about Hyder Ali. You must not mention that name or the British will believe you spy for a man they call a traitor. They have now caught the two Indian thieves who took Sri Ganesha from his place. Our Ganesha is made of lead and only coated in gold paint."

Jan groans. If words could kill, these words seem to strike such a blow to the sahib that he closes his eyes and groans. In the next moments he tells Pearl what she has suspected, that he is one of the thieves who escaped.

"A lead elephant! Of course it had been too heavy. They'd been desperate fools, the batch of them. Fools led astray by the Jew, though perhaps he had not known, otherwise why would he have put his son in danger?"

Jan turns his back to Pearl and his shoulders shake in sobs. "I'm lost. I have led my dearest friend to his death. Let me die, just do not turn me over to the British."

She touches him gently. "I have no love for the British. I've nursed their men, some only boys who told me they were forced onto ships destined for India and made to fight for the Company. No, I do not love the British. I would like to see them all chased from India."

"My best friend killed for a lead idol."

The sahib seems to Pearl as if he would laugh and cry at the same time but that pain prevents him.

"You will wish to live when your strength returns. In the cupboard there is enough rice, brinjal, and onions for several days. I will buy chicken wings for broth to give you strength."

"Look in the lining of my jacket. Yes, cut it open."

Pearl does as he says and from his jacket pour five Star Pagodas.

"The notes are too large and will arouse suspicion. I have coins for the chicken."

"You will keep the Pagodas. Yes, I do wish to continue living. When I feel your gentle touch, it is life calling me."

He grips her hand and her heart pounds. As long as she can remember, Pearl has been forced to lay with men not of her choosing and never loved. The first days when she washed the sahib's body, she traced her fingers to his slim waist and watched as his manhood, thick and rosy-colored against his pale thigh, began to quiver. She touched it lightly and the flesh rose pink with a drop of moisture. How pleasing he must be for a woman, she said to herself, compared to the fat Zamindar and his sickly son, the landowners in the area who paid the temple for her body.

"When I saw your face in the temple pool, I imagined an angel was bringing me to heaven, a destination I have not deserved."

"Do you see my eye?" She turns her face to show him her cursed fate.

"The eye, yes, I noticed. You are a beautiful girl, Pearl, with a kind heart, that is what I see when I look at you."

She falls truly in love from the moment she hears his words and knows her fate will be linked to his.

Pearl changes the dressing on his shoulder that is healing. She speaks to him about his tincture. "Soon the bottle will be empty. I have seen soldiers begging to die for one dose. You must have a strong will and take less and less each day."

Pearl herself has had such terrible opium dreams that she never wished for it again. The habit wasn't common among younger girls, but the older Dasis, afraid of losing their livelihood, take the drug. All of them one day will be told by the priests to unhook their ear pendants and all that will be left to these poor creatures is begging. Auntie is the exception; she is clever and cruel and will live forever.

"I have cured myself before," Jan says. "You would think that a seaman, once he weans himself from the drug would give it up forever, but fears of the sea drive us back to its solace. Do you wish to hear my country's legend of a Dutchman cursed to sail the seas forever until a woman of true heart saves him. I often wonder if it is an opium tale."

"Yes of course, I would like to hear."

She draws near to him and strokes his cheek as he tells her the legend of the Flying Dutchman and the strange ports that he visits but where he cannot rest. Soon he is drowsy and she kisses his eyelids and smoothes hair from his forehead.

"Do you see from the milk eye?" He asks as she spoons chicken broth into his mouth.

"Only light and dark. The people say it's punishment for past lives. Auntie says I have a shell from the sea in the place of an eye that will wash away at the hour of my death. Beware of water, she tells me, which is why I am afraid of the sea and even of rivers."

"Seamen are the most superstitious bunch. We read signs in every-thing. Any one of us still alive should have been swallowed up like Jonah and the whale long ago."

"Who is Jonah?"

"A particularly fortunate man from the Bible." Jan sits up and looks at her. "I have been thinking of the riddle you told me. You are married but do not have a husband?"

"The answer is that a Devadasi born into my community is married to Siva, Lord Nataraja. If I were not cursed with this

milk eye, I might have a protector who keeps me in a fine house, gold bangles, and silk saris but I could not be his wife because I am married, as I just said, to Siva."

"The world is cruel to women who do not have protection from men. I myself was a thief who stole jewels from women I have abandoned."

"Sometimes, I have been so angry when the priests came to me with their dirty business that I placed bits of cow flesh on their lips so in the next life they would be born outcaste also. Shall I tell you my dream?"

"Yes."

"I dream of holding a daughter in my arms who is perfect in every way that I am not."

"You will have a perfect child, Pearl, and perhaps somewhere in the world there is a skilled physician to give you sight in both eyes."

"Do you believe there is such magic?" she asks.

"When we have escaped from here, you will give me a chance to redeem myself by dedicating myself to finding this physician among the Hebrews."

They began to plan their escape. Each week a rice and corn dealer comes to carry food grown in her district to Madras. Pearl will find the man while he is buying onions and brinjals in town. He will take passengers for a price.

"Once we reach Madras," Jan says, " I will hire a boat to take us to Pondicherry that is under French protection. We'll sail on to Ceylon where my countrymen will help us."

"I am afraid of water," Pearl replies.

"There is nothing to fear if we depart before the monsoon and you will be with me."

"Tonight, I will go to the temple to ask my husband Lord Siva for permission to leave him. Then I will dig up Auntie's Star Pagodas."

"Pearl, you cannot believe a stone has a mind or feeling."

"I must go and make a puja or Siva will prevent us from deserting him. Look at the revenge that his son Ganesha brought upon you. I must pray to Sivalingum and leave my earrings before him."

Jan holds his hand over hers and presses it to his heart. "Once we are safely in Madras, I will buy you a pearl necklace like your name and take you as my wife. Bring me my boots, my darling." He twists one heel open and a dozen small sparkling diamonds fell out. "Go now and say your farewells to that god of yours."

Kamala sighed. "This last part came from a dream, Celeste, though I did not smoke opium because I know its dangers for a woman like me."

"You have made such a dramatic story. I will go over it and find words I have missed."

"Can you see Pearl on the cinema screens?"

"I can. I wonder if Pearl's fear of the sea came because I have told you my fears?"

"Do you think so? Perhaps. I have no such fears. Sometimes I do read another's mind."

Celeste thought back on her visit with Salomé and how she'd had a moment of intimation, knowing her friend was going to be in terrible trouble before long. She was not able to say so, and would it have changed Salomé's decision?

"I am fond of Pearl and fear for her safety with Jan. I'm not certain that I trust the man."

"You must beware of Dutchmen. Make a note, Celeste. Dictated January 22, 1976."

17.

Jules woke at five to write during the cool hours when the house stayed quiet, mist still hung on the leaves of mango trees, and Angela slept in the bedroom below. After he'd bought the house, he learned that a Captain Irving had added the Queen Anne turret when he'd retired from the East India Company a century before. Jules neglected the two floors with their vast rooms for entertaining and concentrated on making this top nook his sanctuary study. There he imagined the Captain, a smoker of pipes and drinker of whiskey, reliving his sea battles and exotic ports of call as he composed his memoirs.

In the three months since Angela had begun throwing herself into dance lessons with Kamala Kumari, he had been holding his breath, knowing this quiet hiatus could end any time in a surprise revelation. He didn't trust Kamala's motives but Angela seemed to be thriving so he waited and listened as she played tapes and practiced her steps below. She gave herself over to the discipline and challenge of *bharatanatyam,* the way she had as a child, she told him, learning ballet. Kamala was even talking of a recital. "She wants to show me off as her foreign pupil. There's a competition among teachers for foreigners. She says I'll be the best."

Was Kamala sincere? He'd learned from Suddaraj how he and Celeste had tried to dissuade Angela from her plans to ask Kamala for lessons. According to Celeste, Angela had insisted on meeting the dancer. He trusted Celeste to keep things as calm as possible. She was honest, like Suddaraj. He felt grateful to them both for handling the complications he had created and leaving him free for the important work at hand.

The chance meeting with Sivaram Rao during monsoon in Madurai had set his research and writing in motion. From his ashram, Rao wrote volunteering his services as an assistant. He would gather information about *Devadasis* and translate them. Jules sent him 100 rupees in cash because Rao was prohibited from having personal expenses or a bank account. Rao wrote that he traveled to Tanjore and Trichi to read inscriptions carved into the stone walls of temples and made translations from Tamil, Telegu, and Sanscrit. Every few days, the extraordinary man sent Jules his findings in blue air letters carefully written in green ink. Jules copied all these notes, added questions, posted them back to Rao along with more money for expenses.

"And I am grateful and touched by your interest. You are doing me such good. I have not been wandering nights, no more visits down dangerous alleys in search of chimeras."

"No trouble, Mr. Jules, is too great," Rao wrote. "If I am of help in your vision, that is enough. I am feeling reborn."

Jules organized his chapters and typed them up on his Smith Corona. Most recently, Rao reported discovering the most unusual evidence in the archives of the Rajaraja temple in Tanjore. This document, Rao wrote, listed the rice, land, silk, and jewels granted to individual dancers from the years 1000 to 1010 when the temple must have used *Devadasis* in rituals for the first time. "Merely a few pages of old paper somehow has been preserved there," Rao wrote.

Jules did stop to wonder at the likelihood of paper surviving a thousand years, but it wasn't impossible. The Dead Sea Scrolls had been twice that age when discovered in caves in the desert. The Tanjore temple with its thick stone walls must have protected against climate damage. Another question troubled him: shouldn't this miracle discovery be taken to a museum immediately? For the time being, since Rao wrote he'd replaced all the papers, Jules put his doubts aside. Together, they would write the first true book revealing how the *Devadasi* caste worked, and how injustices built into its existence went to the rotten core of the caste system itself.

Over these weeks, Jules seldom went to his Georgetown office, did not visit the docks, and ignored Rama's sons who were requesting information about shipments through Madras to Jaffna. He had no time to attend to those hotheads, even when they sent letters signed 'anonymous' with threats that he better help or face consequences. The last had read "You promised loyalty to our liberation. Freedom or Death."

———————

As more blue letters came in, Jules sensed something about Rao's language that went beyond scholarship, an intensity that was verging on the imagined scene in a novel or film. Still, it was inspiring how Rao brought dancers and singers of that long-ago past alive, as if they stood before him in all their beauty.

Here is one person called to task for overspending her portion. Against this accusation, she appeals to the priests to advance next month's provision of rice because another Dasi is stealing from her. She complains that a younger person named Star is getting preference in temple duties. There is a dispute. Star wishes to correct the information before a council of priests. Both women use Tamil and Sanscrit maxims, revealing their learning. (Most women of the time were illiterate but Dasis were instructed in music, dance, and classical literature.) There are names of other women such as Pearl, Ruby, and Emerald, Silk, and Gold, not typical Tamil nor Telegu names, but specific to the dancing caste, I would say. These women with their lovely faces and sweet voices may have passed from earth ten centuries ago, but they are speaking to us now lest we forget them. I have felt their shades hovering over me as I sat reading the records of their lives. I am able to smell their sandalwood scent and hear the jingle of their ankle bells, the rustle of their silk pajamas. I follow them into the dark sanctums where foul priests await them to take their pleasure. There I leave them. The life of the mind must remain pure.

I am yours faithfully, M.R .S. Rao.

Rao also wrote personally that Jules was, "the only friend I can tell my troubles to." His eyes followed every young girl, he wrote. He had nighttime emissions after the dream visits of seductive heavenly dancers who used their wiles to tempt him in his sleep. A young woman who worked in the ashram laundry accused him of fondling her but Rao had given her a large packet of sweets and she withdrew her complaint. "I have fasted and cleansed myself, but nothing frees me from my senses. I must keep a strict hold on myself. Is there a chance for me to come to you in Madras to organize your library? In the evening, we shall go to the cinema."

Jules replied that Rao would have a safe and welcome place in his home and a productive routine. Sharing the house with Angela seemed to be going more smoothly than he could have imagined and she wouldn't object to gentle Rao. There were certainly enough rooms for him to have his privacy. One evening, he took Angela to have dinner at Gaylord's Restaurant. It was almost as if he were meeting her for the first time. She was wearing a stunning pale green *salwar Kameez* with green and orange striped pants. In her short hair, she fastened a strand of jasmine behind her ears. Eyes turned when they followed the waiter to the rooftop table. They sat drinking beer and eating chunks of hot, red tandoori chicken with warm, butter-rich naan. Her appetite, her vigor, her charm—she was the girl he had fallen for in New York, only now the lightness had more depth, less uncertainty. He could have fallen in love all over again with those expressive beautiful eyes above the candle light.

They laughed about the Madras Club.

"I know you tried to introduce me because you wanted me to have company." She patted his arm in a confiding matter. "Now, when I run into the women, they say I've gone native, right to my face. There's a nice one, Virginia, but I can't know her without the rest."

"They miss everything worth knowing about life here," he said.

"They didn't have kind words to say about you either."

"Anything in particular?"

"He's gone native, worse than anyone else, they said."

"Is that all?" They laughed.

That night as he passed her room to climb the stairs to his study, he wanted to come in and lie beside her, to confide everything and feel her cool skin against his, but he couldn't without destroying her trust. He knew that he should not disturb her peace.

———————

Voices floated up from below. A door slammed. He stood and went to the window to look down on the driveway where he saw Angela and Celeste getting into a green, older model American car. He could see Kamala Kumari in the front seat beside a driver who was wearing a bill cap. He looked at his watch. Eight in the morning. Why had he not wakened as usual before dawn? Where was Kamala taking them? Before he could descend from his aerie, they were gone and he returned to his desk where two more blue airmail letters and a packet awaited him.

The change in Rao's penmanship struck Jules right away. When they'd first begun corresponding, Rao's cursive letters had moved evenly across the page and his margins kept straight. Now the lines went at uneven angles, letters big and small, ink smudged.

Most respectfully, Sir, I apologize for worries put upon you but you have become the one other person in whom to confide. My nerves are at risk. Temptation entered again my dreams last night. Naked breasts, slender waists, rounded buttocks, beautiful vulvas resulted in this man's sexual exhaustion, female demons waiting for me to lose vigilance.

The letter continued on another page with more legible penmanship, though this time Jules felt Rao's words had an even sadder tone.

Sir, I cannot continue. Scholarship should be a calming influence on men who spend entire lives in a library, but it is causing me illness. The inscription that follows may be your missing piece, the key to open the last doors of the sanctum, while for me it is the portal to madness. Your faithful obedient Rao, will be with you in spirit if destiny should take me from earth. Here are the words transcribed, perhaps my last to you.

The Manikar Came to Dance.

To this day, there is a caste of Manikars in the Tanjore region who perform dramas recounting the life of Krishna. They are valued as wedding guests because they tell the bride her fortune, but women and children are warned to be wary of them: the Manikars have bad reputation for loose morals and stealing girls to join their traveling troupe. I believe you will find that some of the original Dasis are now Manikars. No one else has made this connection. Do not ask more of me. Oh to be done with the source of my tormented body.

Jules paced his study. He knew of the *Manikar* caste, fortune-tellers who often traveled with hermaphrodites and men dressed as women to festivals and weddings. He'd come across a rowdy group wearing heavy make up and garish jewelry on the beach road south of Madras while he was driving in the opposite direction. He asked Suddaraj to slow down so he could watch the bizarrely dressed figures, maybe men, maybe women, thrust their faces toward him. That was close enough. He said, "Drive on." The sound of flute, drum and singing followed for quite a way.

Devadasis turning up as these dissolute *Manikars!* Quite an original idea but it would need documentation, not just figments loosed from Rao's fevered mind. What was he to make of Rao's plea for help? Was he hinting he might do himself harm?

Jules had no telephone number and didn't know precisely the location of Rao's ashram. Should he leave now and take a train to Madurai and from there inquire about a spinning ashram? There could be several. It might take days to find Rao.

Jules realized how tired he felt. His eyes burned and he closed his lids and let his head fall to his desk over the letters.

Within moments he was dreaming he had started his train journey to rescue Rao. Beside him in the carriage sat a woman of indeterminate age wearing a white ermine cape that was open to reveal opulent white breasts. Somehow he reflected that this display was immodest for India and she should cover up. She pointed to her mouth to let him know she was hungry and that he must feed her. Fortunately he had mangoes and the smooth, slick fruit made his own mouth water as he fed her. It didn't surprise him when she whispered in Dutch for him to come closer so she could feed him in return. The soft fold of her fur-trimmed dressing gown was infused with a familiar heavy perfume. She stretched back, exposing veins in her white neck, her throbbing pulse.

"So far from home, my son. Come, beloved son. We are at last alone," she whispered.

"What are you doing here, Mother? I am on a journey of importance to rescue a man."

"There, there, Julie, time to kiss me. I am leaving on the train. There is little time."

"You are on the train. We have all night together."

"Quick, jump from the train and follow me."

"I cannot. I must go on," he replied as the figure began fraying at the edges like a reel of film that caught fire around the edges. He jumped free of the flames.

"I leave you forever now," were the last words he heard.

18.

In the front seat of the car, Kamala was uncorking a thermos of coffee. "We are going south to my village because I have received word that Grandmother has taken a turn for the worse and there's no time to waste. Angela, we'll continue lessons when we return. It is good you see village life to understand India, and Celeste, we are going where I have set Pearl's house and the temple. Seeing them will be useful for story atmosphere and details in nature.

Angela gave Celeste a questioning look.

"Kamala Kumari is writing a story and I am transcribing for her," Celeste said.

"You have so many talents, both of you," Angela said.

"It is Kamala Kumari's imagination. I am only typing words on the machine."

"You're modest, Celeste. You are making me watch my grammar."

On the city outskirts, they passed the tall gates of the Theosophical Society.

"Rukmini Devi teaches there," Kamala said to Angela. "She is a British woman who believes herself to be a reincarnated temple dancer. In England, she learned the "Dying Swan" from Pavlova herself. I have heard that the English woman still fails to understand how dancers had to live in India in previous times, about how we could not be the saints she imagines."

"Lots of people idealize dancers. I show them my feet," Angela said.

Kamala turned to look at Angela. "You understand."

The car jolted them as it left the main highway and drove onto a narrower paved strip where oncoming traffic passed so closely that snatches of music and conversation were sucked in through the open windows. On the side of the road, a barefoot girl, her pregnant belly perfectly egg-shaped, swiveled her head to follow their eyes. As the girl turned, the jug balanced on her head seemed as much part of her as the belly.

"She has the face of a Madonna," Celeste said.

"Village beauties grow old fast. So many children." Kamala said.

"Like our washerwoman, Ravi, at home. She has three babies," Angela said.

"And Suddaraj already has four children he must provide for," Celeste said.

Before noon, Kamala told the driver to stop where lorries were parked and sent him to order vegetarian meals. They would eat on benches in the shade.

Kamala led the way to a small table. The fields smelled of mud, red clods turned over for new planting of rice paddy, still heavy after the monsoon. Water wheels against a pale sky and spidery fishing nets fluttering in the breeze made Celeste homesick for Pondicherry.

A bare-chested boy wearing a black *lungi* brought their banana leaves, scooped portions of rice, yellow *dhal*, and green bean curry with reddish mango pickle on the side. Kamala ate hungrily, and when the boy returned with the pot of *dhal*, she had her leaf refilled. Celeste also accepted more rice. She hoped there would be sweets brought out at the end of the meal. Minutes later, the boy brought *gulab jamun* dripping in sugar.

Kamala smiled as drivers from parked lorries stared. When a handsome young man approached and asked her to sign a paper for his wife, she found a pen in her purse.

She signed with a flourish. "I always please my fans." When the man backed away, Kamala said, "I'm truly happy when I come back to the countryside where people are still innocent and easily satisfied. Yet my heart is sad for the villagers who are so poor."

For the rest of the drive, Celeste drifted between a dream of a heaping plate of milk sweets and waking to find her mouth dry. At some point, the driver had turned off the two-lane road at a Burmah Shell station with red gas pumps. From then on, the car bounced along on gravel and dirt until Kamala told the driver to stop in front of a cluster of small thatched houses.

"You can drive through Tiruchandrum without realizing it," Kamala said.

From descriptions in Kamala's story, Celeste imagined the village larger, more a town. The Red Coats would have been marching in formation on wide streets between houses where people were hiding, but this village was nothing but a rutted dirt path with hunched-over cottages scattered in unkempt brush. She saw they didn't have electricity poles nor phone lines. She wouldn't be able to call Sahib Jules to tell him where Angela had gone. She sighed over the complications Kamala got her into.

Two barefoot boys wearing raggedy shorts ran to the car and touched the hot metal, then jumped back blowing on their fingers.

"Mostly young people have all gone. No one is working here and no dancing masters are teaching young girls their steps. In the old days, you could hear our feet keeping time and the ring of our ankle bells. I do not know how these boys live and who they belong to," Kamala said.

A very old woman drowsing in the shade of a doorway woke up at the sound of the car.

"Mahadevu!" Kamala leaned out of the window. "Driver, pull over and park in a shady spot. And Celeste, you stay with Angela while Mahadevu and I go to Grandmother. Sandwiches and Orange Squash are in the hamper. Walk around to get an idea of the village."

Kamala got out and knelt before the old woman, touching her feet.

"Let's walk. We've been sitting a long time and that road was bumpy," Angela said.

"Put on your hat, Missy. The sun is so bright and hot in the countryside."

Except for the two boys who followed them, they met no other person, not even a keeper of the white-washed temple. Celeste led Angela around the back to see if there was a pond. There, sunk in muck and algae, lay a tank with only a scum of turgid water at the bottom. Had a gold-painted Ganesha really been here when people lived in this poor village?

The heat made them stagger back to the car where they climbed in and drank the warm sodas. They were too hot to talk for long, and stretched out in the front and back seats. The driver seemed to have disappeared. They closed their eyes and fell asleep. .

They slept until Kamala came and woke them. The sun had set and though it wasn't entirely dark, the half moon risen over the temple shone like a beacon. Kamala had a ghostly smear of ash on her forehead. Her eyes were wet with tears and kohl ran down her cheeks.

"Grandmother has died peacefully. I arrived just in time to take her hand and receive her blessing before she breathed her last. Now I must wait while women prepare her body. We will go back to Mahadevu. She will tell her lover that she must help lay out Grandmother and won't be able to meet him later. Her lover is eighty or more years and comes every night from his home to see her. He is a Chettiyar landowner who has a wife and family of his caste, but he and Auntie also have grandchildren together. The Chettiyar's land will go to his wife's family, not a rupee to Mahadevu, but she believes that in the next life they will be husband and wife. Do you believe in Karma, Angela?"

"I don't know. Do you, Teacher?" Angela asked.

"Yes, of course I do. Celeste does not believe, however."

"We Christians believe Jesus will return to save sinless people."

"Who is without sin? There must be very few who are admitted to heaven," Kamala said.

At that moment, Mahadevu beckoned them to her house. She was very small and wrapped in a homespun cream sari with a blue cloth over her shoulders. Kamala again knelt at the old woman's bare feet, then the two of them pressed their foreheads together, silently crying.

"Come, sit on the mats," Kamala said. Celeste and Angela lowered themselves to the floor. "She wishes to serve you tea before he comes."

Mahadevu rattled china cups with her shaking hands. Celeste spooned lots of sugar into her tea, realizing how thirsty and hungry she was. Angela also heaped sugar.

Mahadevu peered out her window. Dogs began barking down the

lane. Mahadevu rushed to a mirror to rub color from a small pot onto her cheeks. On each side, she left a round patch of red.

They tried not to look at each other, but Angela and Celeste had to bite their tongues to keep from laughing.

The door opened as if by a stream of moonlight.

"Her lover for sixty years," Kamala whispered. "He comes only at night."

A figure in white pajamas drifted in as if carried by the moon-light. When Celeste saw the man's face, tiny and brown as a nut, she couldn't stand it any longer. Angela seemed to lose control at the same moment. They ran out the open door, doubled over against a wall, and covered their mouths. They were about to run for the car like guilty children, when Kamala Kumari caught Celeste by the shoulder.

"You are shameless, both of you. Where is your respect?"

"I'm sorry. We couldn't help ourselves. They are such old people. I'm sorry," said Celeste.

"But you two are not so young to lack respect. Fortunately they only see each other and are mostly deaf. And now you will come to pay respects to Grandmother. Please act properly."

They found themselves in a room with four old women who were engaged in washing a tiny, naked body that looked as if it had been shrunk like the kind of mummy Celeste had seen pictures of in books, but never so exposed. She had to force herself to concentrate on the nearly bald head puckered like a dried apple, oiled and colored with saffron and turmeric, rather than let her eyes look at the rest of the naked body. The four women continued to pour fluids over the body and then sprinkled turmeric powder as if Kamala's grandmother were a chicken being readied for the oven. Celeste had been to wakes for *Soeurs* and priests who were fully dressed in their habits, only hands and powdered faces showing. A Christian would never expose the woman's privates, smooth and hairless as a newborn. A *Soeur* was carried to the cathedral graveyard with the modesty of a virgin.

Kamala and then Mahadevu joined the women as they bound the corpse's hands together with more flowers and propped up the chin. Kamala placed drops of oil on her grandmother's eyelids and leaned down to kiss them. The women then wound the body in white cloth, covered the mound with roses, jasmine and marigolds.

At the door, the two small boys they had seen on the road came in carrying a palm litter that they set down next to the corpse. As they were about to lift the flower-decked body onto it, Kamala rushed forward. "No! No! Do not take her away," she cried. "Do not take Amma from me. Let her remain a few moments longer."

Kamala went to her knees. The boys waited. They were so thin, so meager, that Celeste wondered if they could lift the body and all the flowers, but then they did, and carried it toward the door. Kamala followed. Celeste and Angela let themselves out and hurried toward the car.

"I've never been quite so close to a dead person. She looked preserved," Angela said.

"Like a mummy," Celeste said.

"Like a mummy, just what I was thinking, but to be naked! That is really strange."

"The Hindus are strange to me as well, as if I came from another country," Celeste said. "I have seen the very old and peaceful *Souers* who didn't fear death but they would have been terrified if in death their clothes were to be emoved for all to see."

Kamala appeared, her face and top of her head covered in ash. "Where is the driver?"

"We don't know," they answered together.

"I must find him. He must take us home."

They waited until Kamala arrived with the driver who she pushed forward toward the car. He looked unsteady on his feet.

"He's been drinking palm wine. I hope he can drive. Please start the car," Kamala commanded. The driver turned the key and right away drove them off the road into paddy stubble.

"Do I have to slap you!" Kamala batted the back of his head.

"No, Miss, I shall drive."

———

No other car headlights, nothing but moonlight and paddy field surrounded them until they reached the larger road with the Burmah Shell station that Celeste recognized.

"You must turn here!" Kamala again swatted the back of the driver's head.

———————

Celeste knew she'd been dozing because she hadn't seen anything before she felt and heard a crash, saw an arc of light rise up before them and sink back down. She heard the awful sound of Kamala's head thrown back, then forward, as if a bone cracked.

She pushed open her door and stepped outside to see what had happened. Right away, she saw the damaged front of the car, the headlights' broken glass on the pavement and a guard rail smashed in the middle. Then she heard a cry. Ahead, by the light of someone's torch, melons as big as yellow balls were rolling down the road to where her eyes fell on a twisted bicycle. A boy was lying beside the cycle. The melons were still rolling down the slope off the road as the bicycle wheels turned in the air.

People were emerging from the darkness and making a circle around the boy and his bicycle. She saw the unnatural angle of his leg in khaki shorts, and then she saw bone, white against dark skin.

A man came running up. "Someone fetch a doctor for this child. Who will bring a doctor?"

Kamala had her head in her hands and was moaning. Their driver was gone.

"Thanks to God we are not badly hurt. Missy, you are all right?"

"Yes, I'm fine. We must see to that boy." Angela had also stepped from the car.

Celeste walked back to the people standing around the boy and asked if anyone could take him and her mistress to a hospital in Madras where they would be cared for.

A taxi driver stepped forward. "Let us carry the boy first."

"They shouldn't move him, it will only make it worse," Angela said, but people already had lifted him, groaning and crying, into the front beside the taxi driver to leave room for the women.

"Someone must know his family," one man said. "Go fetch mother or father. Which hospital will you be going to, Miss?"

"Lady Wellington." Kamala managed to raise her head.

They helped Kamala to the taxi and squeezed together in the back seat.

"Cross the bridge and go slowly. Soon we'll reach Lady Wellington Hospital," Celeste directed when she saw the pillared white building behind a gate.

At that moment, Kamala called out, "Jules, where are you?"

Angela gripped Celeste's arm. "What is she saying? Why is she saying my husband's name?"

"Missy, she has hit her head."

"I know that, but how many men with that name do we know?"

"Jules, Jules," Kamala moaned.

"Turn there, into the circle, Driver. Missy, come, we'll fetch the doctor. He will pay more respect if you are beside me."

They ran up a flight of stairs to a landing where a nurse stopped them.

"Where is Doctor?" Celeste asked.

"Doctor not to be disturbed." The nurse tried to stop them but they pushed past.

"Doctor is sleeping. He will be angry."

"We'll have to wake him up. There's been an accident. We have brought a boy with a badly broken leg and a woman who has hit her head," Angela said.

Celeste and Angela smelled the whiskey fumes that filled the warm air as a lumbering figure, a man wearing only an undershirt and trousers, came toward them.

"What in bloody hell are you doing!"

"Pardon, Sir. There's been an accident." Angela stepped forward and the doctor paused.

"I am the wife of Jules Van Steen. You are Dr. Fitzgerald."

"So, this is that man's wife. You've gotten over the fever?"

"Yes. We have injured passengers in the car outside. Will you see them?"

"Where are they? In a car did you say?"

"In the taxi. Both are injured."

"I'm coming. Nurse, where is my coat?"

"That doctor is drunk, as bad as the driver. He can't help us," Angela said.

"We put ourselves in his hands. The Sahib doctor will know what to do."

A few minutes later, Dr. Fitzgerald came back out dressed in a white coat. When he opened the back seat of the car, Kamala looked up at him.

"You will help me, Doctor."

"What about the boy! His leg is very bad." Celeste tugged on the doctor's coat.

"Will you desist, girl? I'll send someone. It's probably fakery, for money."

"No, his bone is through the skin. He is in the most need."

"All in good time, girl. Now step aside while I assist the lady."

19.

Celeste returned to Lady Wellington Hospital where she waited patiently until Sister Sheba came to tell her that Kamala's injuries were not serious. "A mild concussion and scalp-line lacerations. Doctor has already told Miss Kumari that healing will be complete, with no scars. She is resting comfortably."

"That's good news. When can I see her?" Celeste smoothed her skirt and patted her hair after her bike ride. "I'm a personal secretary to Miss Kumari."

"Our patient has made a request to see no visitors at present," Sister Sheba replied.

Celeste blushed with embarrassment. She wouldn't argue because that would show hurt feelings but she felt dismissed as just another applicant to see Kamala Kumari.

She bicycled back under a broiling sun to the Sahib's where she didn't know what awaited her. Would the Sahib be there? Her Missy? They had accompanied the injured boy taken to Madras General Hospital after Dr. Fitzgerald refused to admit him, but they hadn't spoken since.

The expression on Angela's face at the door showed that no more concealing was possible.

"Celeste, come in and let's have a cool drink and talk."

She followed Angela into the downstairs room the where most of the work had been done to clean and repair. There was a sheen of white paint that made the room light.

"Have you seen her?" Angela asked.

"I went to call at the hospital but she is saying no visitors."

"Not even you?"

"No, but she is not in any danger. The nurse said only superficial cuts."

"You've been at her beck and call," Angela said. "I'm surprised she didn't see you."

"Missy, I never found a way to tell you that I knew in the past the Sahib and Kamala Kumari had been friends."

"So they were lovers?"

"Certainly they knew each other well. I do not know more."

"Have they re-commenced knowing each other well since I've been here?"

Celeste vigorously shook her head. "Oh no, not even once that I know of."

"How do you know that? Are you with her every moment?"

"No, Missy, but Kamala has another friend and she believes that Sahib has betrayed her."

"With me? That's got to be upsetting to her pride. I didn't take him away. Maybe I got him to help me out of a jam but that's not the same. It's their high romance, not mine."

Celeste stood up. "May I have a drink of water. It is very hot outside now."

"Sorry," Angela said.

They went into the dark kitchen where the cook sat in a corner stirring a pot on a kerosene burner. Celeste knew he was cooking for his own family who lived in the back in a shed within the garden. She also knew Ravi the washerwoman did her own family laundry with the Sahib's soap but these were the kind of things that poor people always did when a vigilant housewife didn't keep an eye out.

They went to sit again in the cool large room shaded from the sun by new long blinds. "I hope you understand that I don't need to know about Jules' life before we met, though learning about Kamala might have helped me understand his indifference."

"I am sure Sahib cares for you."

"But he doesn't desire me. That's all right, I won't embarrass you."

Angela touched Celeste's arm. "I only wish you'd told me instead of concealing what you knew."

"I tried not to lie, Missy. There never seemed a good time to speak of it."

"You're such a good person. It must have been difficult."

"I hated concealing." Celeste lowered her eyes. "Missy, I understand very little about a person such as Kamala. She acts without thinking. Suddaraj says her nature is fire, which makes sense to me."

"I told you intimate things. I told you about pills I took."

"I know, Missy. And of course I have not said a word but I should have told you from the first night you wished to go to meet Kamala Kumari. I said nothing about her bungalow."

"Her bungalow! I don't know about a bungalow. Did they meet there?"

"Sahib gave it to her but he never comes. She goes with another man, the one with the car."

"If you'd told me would I have thrown myself at her feet? Would I have seen how she pretended to teach me dance but was using me for her own purposes, maybe revenge?"

"You had in your mind to know her and to learn dance. You became a pupil who excels. I know she respects you."

"What am I to believe?" Angela looked down at her feet. "I've been happy to be a pupil but we could have avoided all the small lies and insinuations she's made if you had spoken up and given me the choice to continue or not."

"I'm sorry, Missy. I was not brave to do so. I have failed."

"I care about you, Celeste, and I do understand you've been caught in the middle. It's mostly my pride that's hurt. I don't know what to do next but I feel calm about it, not like I did months ago when Jules swept me off to Madras."

"You have talked with Sahib Jules?"

"He said what you have told me, that they had broken off their relations but that he should have spoken. He did not try to pretend he had no feelings for her. I'm glad he could be that honest."

"I am sure that Sahib is regretting his situation."

"I'm not his only problem. There's a group of crazy young men in Ceylon he doesn't want to talk about, and another friend who's perhaps gone crazy, that he blames himself for. I'm worried about the boy we left in the hospital ward. At home, we could bring charges against Dr. Fitzgerald for neglect but I suppose not here."

"Doctors set the broken leg and Suddaraj has located the family. Kamala must give the father rupees to buy food while the boy cannot work. Suddaraj with bring the money."

"I will get cash from Jules and leave it at the YWCA for you to give the boy."

"It is kind of you, Missy, not to be more angry. Perhaps you will forgive one day."

Angela's eyes teared, and so did hers. "I am grateful to you, Celeste. You are my friend. Maybe I'm more embarrassed than anything to be seen as a fool."

"I do not see you as any fool. More myself, likely. Suddaraj and I tried to talk you out of the dancing but you are not sorry you have been her pupil?"

"No, not at all. Was Kamala intending to embarrass me, do you think?"

Celeste shook her head. "I don't believe so. She wishes to impress the American. She said that you learned the Indian style so quickly and well."

"Celeste, I'm going to quietly think this out. Thank you. I'll see you tomorrow?"

As she walked to get on her bicycle, Celeste saw Suddaraj in the doorway. He waved to her and smiled his beautiful smile. Suddaraj seemed to know what she was feeling.

Moments later, Angela came to the door as if she wanted to call back the figure disappearing at the end of the drive.

"Baba cares very much for you, Memsahib. I also am to blame," Suddaraj said.

"I don't blame her or you, Suddaraj. You two have been my real friends. We've all been close together."

"Yes, Missy. I have been enjoyed the best times of friendship of my life."

"I've decided to leave the house and go to a hotel. I'll miss you both."

"Hotel, Memsahib? Not alone?"

"Yes, alone."

Suddaraj began to protest that it wouldn't look right, but Angela put her hands to her lips and shook her head. "Don't worry. Just find me a nice quiet hotel where there isn't a British crowd. The last people I want to see are Sahibs and Memsahibs. You and Celeste can visit me there."

He couldn't find the words to tell his mistress how impossible her idea was but he'd never been able to argue with a woman. His wife, Meena, who was barely four feet tall, had a will that dominated his own. She was also a fire woman, like Kamala Kumari, though they looked nothing alike. Meena had a little round face, a snub nose with two ruby chips in each side. Sitting on the ground chopping vegetables, grinding spices, she could be taken for a child though she had borne four children. Baba was not like either of these women. She was tender and touched his heart in a way he could not explain.

"Suddaraj, are you listening? I'm going to pack up my few things now. Will you drive me to find a hotel and bring my bike later?"

"Sahib is a good man, Missy. He will be sad bachelor alone." Suddaraj looked at his feet.

"He's certainly not a bad man. He's kind to you, very fair, not like a lot of Europeans I've met. Wait, I've changed my mind. I'd like my bike if you'll please tie it on the back of the car so I'll have it at the hotel when I get there."

––––––––––

During the days that followed, Celeste found the only place she felt both peaceful and cool was Higginbothams where she went for a new volume or to talk with Rangan. He offered tea and stories of famous writers who had come into Higginbothams. She told him how different and strange it had been to read about young boys and their schooling in *Swami and Friends,* the small novel he'd recommended on the first visit to the book store.

"For one thing, I have never known boys who are so much bolder than we girls were." She stopped for a moment to think. "No, that's not entirely correct. My friend, Salomé, who you met the first time I came, was bold enough to run away with no prospects in this big city. Without her I wouldn't have come. Girls are bold in different ways, I guess."

"Yes, I remember a fair girl who did not seem happy in a book store, while I saw in you from the beginning that many books would be yours." Rangan laughed. 'I do not mean that I singled you out as a customer, but as a real *reader*."

"Not only are they boys who are Swami's friends, but they are not Christian."

"Does that trouble you?" Rangan asked.

"No, but what troubled was how ignorant the Christian teachers were about these boys, not respecting the Hindus. It makes me realize that giving respect is most important in life."

"Ever since I began reading, ignorance only seems greater," Rangan said. 'Especially of Christians, as I am Hindu myself, so I am on a reading assignment to understand Mr. Graham Greene, who, by the way, was the first British to further R.K. Narayan's career abroad, and only then, appreciation came in India."

"That is interesting. But you are not ignorant. You are well read," she said.

"Perhaps one day I will know from Socrates onward. So little time, so much to read."

"And I wish I could stay here in a chair with books all day, but I must return to people who are not so humble in their ignorance, if I may say so. Nor so quiet. They are always making a lot of trouble for themselves and for me."

"May I inquire what has been your means of livelihood, Miss Celeste?"

"I began cleaning rooms at the Connemara Hotel where my friend found a position, and she had me take lessons on doing hair and nails. When I moved to work in the salon, I was asked to take private employment with a Sahib and his wife who is from America, and also with a film actress. I am often with this actress, and recently I am taking dictation and typing a story she is composing in her head. Somehow I am able to manage."

"You are having experience for a book of your own," he said. "Next time you visit, perhaps you shall tell me more detail about your life."

"And you will tell me about yourself, if you don't mind."

"There is not much. I am a bachelor, who, since I have passed my B.A. and left college, am back living with family, where there are very many people who give me no privacy to read because they consider my reading a waste of time and money since I keep my light burning late at night. I have my little peace here in Higginbothams. Sometimes a person comes and we talk as you and I do."

"I would give up my jobs to work in a bookshop or a library. It would be more peaceful than what I am doing now," she said.

A ring on the door signaled a customer. "Well, not every moment is heaven, because there are customers. It has been a pleasure to talk with you, Miss Celeste. Come back soon." Rangan looked into her eyes before they both hurried away, he to his customer and she back into the waves of heat rising from the pavement on Mount Road.

20.

A boy in khaki showed Angela a room at the Das Prakash that opened onto a view of an extensive, lush garden behind the hotel. The room had a double bed under a white cover, air-conditioning and a full-length mirror to practice in front of.

"It's perfect. Please tell the desk that I'll pay for a week and decide on more."

The boy nodded. "But you must come to sign, Memsahib."

"I shall. I'm glad it's on the top floor so I won't bother anyone. Thank you."

She changed from a skirt and blouse into the *salwar kameez* with loose trousers she used to work out, and for an hour, practiced steps to the recording Kamala had made for her. Then she showered, called below to ask for her bicycle to be brought to the front gate. On the way out, she signed the guest book and gave the name of Jules' bank. "They will pay immediately," she said.

Even at five in the evening, the sun still shone very hard in her eyes as she cycled over the Poonamallee Bridge, along College Road. She followed signs for "Hospital" until she reached the crescent drive of Lady Wellington. Up a flight of steps and inside, she caught the nurse by surprise.

"I wish to see Miss Kamala Kumari."

Sister Sheba led her down the hall to a large room with windows letting in a golden light.

Kamala's bandages rested loosely on her head like a decorative turban. Her eyelids were slightly swollen, but otherwise, three days after being thrown forward and hitting her head so hard on the seat, she looked comfortably languorous rather than invalided.

"I am feeling peaceful here. They give me tinctures to help me sleep. I'm having the first good rest in months. Only the nurses object that observing mourning for Grandmother over eleven days without bathing is not sanitary, but I must do this my way."

A smell of body sweat and gin wafted from Kamala's bedside, mixing with floral scents of roses and gardenias in bouquets.

"Are you still planning the dance demonstration for the Americans that you asked me to be part of?" Angela asked. "I've been practicing the *tillana*."

"Good, continue your practice of *tillana*. How is your large home?"

"I'm staying at the Das Prakash."

Kamala sat up. "You are not at the College Road house?"

"No."

Kamala seemed to think about a further question but instead, picked up a small book from her bedside table. "Have you read the French writer, Miss Colette? All about the French intrigues with love. The novel is called *Cheri* and it is very interesting how a man cannot forget a woman."

"I am not a reader like Celeste. I hoped we could talk about the performance and what it is that you want of me now, if anything."

Kamala yawned. "What would I want of you? I am so tired that I must get more rest but you must practice. The Das Prakash? Not First Class is it? Your husband doesn't pay for the best. He could have you staying at the Connemara."

"I would hate the Connemara. I am making my own decisions."

"Congratulations. I have been making these choices out of necessity all my life."

Angela bicycled back down College Road, pumping hard up to the bridge; the fierce heat seemed to whip her anger hotter, as did all the bright colors, red and purple bougainvillea. How patronizing Kamala had been, she thought, barely noticing that she'd reached the crest of the rise and was heading downhill so fast toward the Das Prakash that she could barely hold onto the handlebars. She swerved to avoid the gate, turned around, dismounted and gave a peon her bike.

Once in her room, she turned on the shower and drenched herself in cold water, dried off and lay down under the fan where she slept until the phone on her bedside table rang.

"A Memsahib Virginia. She wishes to meet in the garden cafe."

Though the sun had gone down, the garden looked wilted, palm leaves lusterless and dusty, bougainvillea bleached out. Angela glanced around for Virginia, but didn't see her. Beneath a nearly leafless tree a pair of goats were standing and staring at her like two bearded old men. A fat man at a table was molding rice balls from his plate and throwing them into his mouth with such detachment she was surprised at his accuracy. Beside him sat a small woman hidden in a sari to the tip of her nose. She fed bites to herself and a baby on her lap. An older girl in a short pink ruffled dress chewed biscuits and smiled at Angela. Angela smiled back and drank her sweet yogurt drink.

"Angela!"

A thin woman wearing a flowered dress that seemed to hang on her frame, her face hidden by dark glasses and a floppy hat, stopped at the table. Angela stood up.

"Where were you?" Virginia asked.

"Virginia? I came into the garden. You must have been waiting for me in the lobby and I passed by. You've lost so much weight I hardly recognize you. Sit down, please."

"Are you really staying in this Indian place? I don't see anybody but natives."

"I have a large cool room upstairs. People are all nice to me."

"You're putting on a good face, I know it, but you don't need to hide your broken heart from me, Angela. You are my sister in sorrow now." Virginia took her arm in a tight grip and squeezed. "Poor us, the two of us abandoned in god-awful India together."

Angela shook Virginia's hand free. "I am fine here, thank you.

What about you?"

She's feverish, Angela thought, and half out of her mind. On her cheeks, she'd painted two clownish spots of color over her makeup. Maybe the other women had ganged up on her.

"Virginia, let me order a *lassi* for both of us. The yoghurt cools you down."

"I don't eat, I don't sleep." Virginia stubbed out her cigarette and started to light another. "In the day, there are the children, but at night I'm in hell. Douglas went off with that Gita person. She's a half-caste who's a secretary for your awful husband. Douglas says he's been in love with her for years. In love! She's dark, for God's sake, a brown woman! He can have her without love, but he's asking for divorce so they can marry in Australia. Giving up everything, leaving his babes behind for a whore."

"I'm so sorry." Angela reached across and took Virginia's hand.

"I'll wait for him, yes I will." Virginia squeezed Angela's fingers, let them go and wiped her eyes behind the dark glasses. "At least you know what being deserted is like. You're the only one who is suffering the way I am."

"I'm not as unhappy as you imagine."

"Didn't yours betray you as Douglas betrayed me?"

"I wonder how you found out? I've been here only a day."

"There are no secrets you can keep here. We're all in this together."

"I'm not in this with anyone except a few friends."

"I saw the girl you used to bring everywhere with you, the servant girl with dark skin and a saucy tongue. She was in the booksellers on Mount Road of all places, chatting up one of the clerks. I asked if she could read and she raised her eyebrows. Cheeky thing. I got it out of her where you were, told her it was an emergency."

Virginia's eyes started to fill with tears she wiped at with a napkin. "I heard about your man and that woman, but I wouldn't have said anything until now."

"You knew about which woman?"

"Don't you remember at the club when we warned you about Indian women of her type? Then you started the dance nonsense with all those wiggling arms and legs."

Angela laughed. "There's something to lots of difficult wriggling that I enjoy. Have you ever seen modern dance? They wiggle, too. And the woman you mean became my teacher."

"Your teacher! You mean you knew what went on between them and you became a student of that dirty dance? Maybe you liked that kind of thing."

Angela looked down to hide a smile, then signaled the waiter. "Two *lassis*, please."

"Douglas' native whore was your husband's secretary. I already said that. I wonder if you knew all about that as well."

"Virginia, I had no idea about any of this. I never met his secretary. I had no hint of my husband's activities either. That's the truth."

Virginia nodded. "I believe you."

"Thank you."

"I was sure the English babies would hold Douglas. I don't understand how he can be transferring to the branch in Australia. He'll never be chairman of the company and he won't see his children. The woman has half a dozen brats of her own. They'll have a disgusting mulatto crew, and his career is finished." Virginia's body shook with tears.

"Here, Ginny, drink some *lassi*. It's cool and you'll feel better."

"Australia. Tell me the truth. Would you have vamped Douglas if he'd made eyes at you?"

Angela felt a flush of anger. "What are you talking about, Virginia?"

"Douglas thought you were stunning."

"Frankly, I don't remember Douglas or anyone from one night at your club."

"He told me you were cute as a French actress. He wanted to dance with you, but didn't dare ask. I hated imagining you with him."

"Virginia, you're torturing yourself with fantasies."

"Douglas was my life, my love. I might as well finish myself off. It's over."

"You will not say that again." Angela took her arm. "You cannot let your children know you think this. Take them back to England. Don't you have family there?"

"What nearly did me in was that Douglas still made love to me when he came home, after he'd been with her. Douglas was always the sexiest man."

"You'll simply have to push those thoughts and feelings away and get practical."

"You're an ice princess. You don't even hear me."

"I do hear you. I'll go home soon myself. Why would you stay in Madras?"

Virginia seemed not to have heard. "I'll follow them to Australia. I'll get brown all over and stay thin. He can have me on the side." She lit another cigarette "Leave this dirty hotel and come stay with me, Angela. We'll make each other feel better. You'll be with your own people."

Angela lowered her eyes. "Thank you but I need to be on my own."

"I don't know how to be on my own!" Virginia picked up her dark glasses and her bag. "You always thought I was a stupid cow."

"No, I felt you are the kindest of all, Virginia. You can come talk any time."

Virginia shook her head, grabbed her purse and glasses, and ran from the terrace.

21.

"I am reaching the conclusion in my mind," Kamala said from the bed. "Are you managing without me? Plenty of free time, I suppose. Have you been to the bungalow, Celeste?"

"The Sahib has been paying into my account at Barclay's. I have been at the YWCA and not the bungalow. Would you like me to go there?"

"Yes, please go and type up the new pages I shall dictate. You don't wish to stay there, though it is so much nicer than the Y?"

"I do not have the love for the sea that you do. I would not want to be alone there."

"But now, when you hear this part of the story, you will see how I have taken your fears into consideration and turned them into art. There's not much time, so let us begin."

Celeste sat for the next hour taking Kamala's dictation.

When Kamala finished, Celeste didn't know what to think. The story had taken such a strange turn.

"Please come back late this afternoon to help me pack, and bring polish for my fingernails. And, here, take money and add it to your account. I won't be outdone by any Sahib."

After Celeste left, Kamala rested and then applied make up and tied her hair into a knot with flowers from a bouquet at her bedside. Dr. Ian Fitzgerald would be coming soon to play a hand of cards. She would have to tell him this was their last morning together.

Kamala dealt a hand of Hearts and won a shot of gin that Fitzgerald prepared with lemon squash. The doctor got up, went to add ice from a small fridge installed in Kamala's room. As he shuffled for another hand, her bedside telephone rang.

"You must forgive me." She picked up the receiver. "Thank you, Auntie, I will be happy to see you. Yes, I am fully recovered and ready to be released. I owe it all to my dear doctor." She smiled and replaced the phone. "Dear Ian, continue recounting your daring exploits crossing the Khyber Pass with the Rajput regiment."

Dr. Ian Fitzgerald had heard a male voice on the line and bristled at being made a fool, but he did as she wished, cleared his throat and took a drink "From all viewpoints, the partition of India was one bloody disaster. We in the medical profession were the first to open trains from the Punjab during the riots. Corridors ran with blood. Yet little ones as brave as Kim himself survived."

"I know one of those children who survived. The dreadful memories haunt him more than the scars he carries," Kamala said.

"Who is the poor fellow?"

"A family friend, a much older man."

"After those bloody months in 1947, I'd had enough of India and took a posting home to visit my mother's grave and see my sisters in County Cork. My youth was gone and what had I to show for it? No family but what remained in Ireland, all ignorant as lambs of what I had seen."

"You never married. You must have been a devilish handsome fellow." Kamala looked directly into bloodshot blue eyes.

"Truth is, the daughters of colonels were a snobbish lot. English are terrible snobs, you know that. I never gave or received a heart. After a visit to Paris, I'd had my fill of the continent's sinful spots and took up doctoring here in the backwater south of the country."

"We have culture and taste, but Prohibition is such a bother," she said.

"Natives do have less tolerance for alcohol—yourself excepted. You drink like a trooper and never seem the worse for it. For an old man, I still hold the liquor."

"You're not old, Ian." Kamala stroked the doctor's puffy palm, turned over his hand that was soft, pinkish, and patterned with liver spots.

When the doctor was called to attend an emergency that had just been brought in, Kamala opened a second small book by Colette, *The Vagabond*. The first sentence struck deep as if a bell being rung at a great distance had been intended for her to hear.

"*Yes, this is the dangerous, lucid hour. Who will knock at the door of my dressing-room, what face will come between me and the painted mentor peering at me from the other side of the looking-glass? Chance, my master and my friend, will, I feel sure, deign once again to send me the spirits of his unruly kingdom.*"

The lines sent shivers down her back. Thank heavens Hari had called to ask for the evening. A night with Hari, no questions and no talk, only love making, was what she needed most.

She got up from the bed and went into the adjoining bathroom. She ran her own bath, let it fill half way and submerged. This time she scrubbed because she had not bathed for the eleven days after her grandmother's death. Now was the time to cleanse the body. As she oiled her hair, she heard Nurse Sheba in the hall.

"Celeste, don't stand out there talking about me!" Kamala called out.

"I am coming. I just heard that a Memsahib has taken many pills and the doctor is doing his best to save her. It seems such a terrible sin to wish to end life before God wishes it. Nurse said the cause was her husband who is leaving her and children for another woman. I think I know which Memsahib it is. I spoke recently with her."

"What a pity to give a man the satisfaction of that! If she dies, he has gotten off without punishment. Was she well acquainted with my pupil?"

"I think if a man knew that his wife had died for him, it would be punishment forever. My Missy knew her, yes, but I don't believe they were well acquainted."

"You are romantic, like our films. My Missy this, my Missy that. Enough of all these women. You tell me which sari shall I choose? Red georgette with gold arrows? Green silk? Why don't you wear saris? You can choose one of mine. Even this Missy you love so much doesn't wear frocks."

"I'm used to frocks. I might try trousers, like foreign girls, for the comfort."

"Trousers! What a horror! Nothing shows a woman's figure to advantage as well as the sari. Frocks are ill-fitting and pants worse. Did you bring polish for my nails, dear girl?"

Celeste worked on cuticle, then nails, reshaping, buffing, and then painting with the scarlet polish Kamala preferred.

"Celeste, can you recreate the hair design from *Veiled for Love*? All these troubles have made me lose some thickness. Raj Tewari brought me several hair pieces."

Celeste piled a coil of artificial black hair into Kamala's chignon, wove in jasmine and roses.

"You are such a clever girl. I count on your help in preparation for our travels. You should be showing gratitude for the opportunity I am giving."

"I am grateful, Kamala. I am only now believing my good fortune."

Kamala looked in the mirror and began to outline her eyes in kohl, then applied a green shadow to her lids. "I wonder if the little American has been keeping up, or if she'll be quite unrehearsed because she is no longer interested."

"Miss Angela is practicing every day in her hotel."

"You see her then? She knows we are leaving for Bombay and Paris? That we have been invited and our expenses all paid so that I may show our dance to French and Americans?"

"I will tell her, Kamala, but I have not seen her since she moved into Das Prakash."

"She will envy you, isn't that good? Imagine, you and I shall be seeing France where you will speak the language."

Kamala stretched her hands toward the ceiling, placed them over her head and moved her neck back and forth with her eyes going the opposite direction.

"I am feeling more optimistic than in many years. The accident did me greater good than harm." Kamala tied the red sari tightly and perfumed herself with Tabu.

Two nurses poked their heads in the door, then jumped aside as heavy footsteps came crashing down the corridor.

"Am I the last to hear the news! Damn your eyes, woman, you're dressed like a streetwalker." Dr. Fitzgerald looked disheveled in his white surgical gown

Kamala turned the rings on her fingers. "I must pay my bill."

"Damn the bill. I will swallow the bill. You are disobeying orders."

"You have been marvelous company and taken such care of me. I could listen to all of *Kim* and *The Man Who Would be King* from the beginning all over again."

"Then why leave me?" Fitzgerald glared out the window. "You have no need of all that paint to enhance your attractiveness."

"You men never know how we perform our magic on you."

"If I were younger, I'd give a beating to the man who is going to entertain you tonight. Best not to think of it." Fitzgerald poured himself Scotch.

"Come here, Ian. Sit by me." She pulled his speckled hand to her and held it. "You've made me feel like a pampered girl and taken worries from me. Men have treated me in many ways, but never so gently and kindly. I will remember our conversations. I have been telling Celeste here what a film story your life would make."

Celeste, who had backed into a corner and was trying to make herself unseen, nodded.

His hands shook as he lifted his drink. "I forget how a woman can brighten the day. This place will be dull without you. I'm a bargain compared to that Dutchman who cannot keep his trousers up. The man's a hopeless case and will only cause you to come to grief."

"I have no intention of setting eyes on the man again, be assured of that, Ian."

Fitzgerald's Indian assistant knocked softly on the door. He ignored it until the knocking increased and the voice said, "Sir, British woman admitted for overdose of sleeping medication, Tire company manager's wife, calls for you."

"I heard that a Memsahib was foolish," Kamala said.

"She'll pull through. A call for help but she won't get attention from that bounder of a husband. Please wait, I'll return as soon as I calm her down."

———————

Ian Fitzgerald didn't arrive in time to stop Kamala from leaving. He stood at his window and watched her enter a car, fanning his hot cheeks and chewing lemon rinds to cover the smell of alcohol. So much sorrow in the world, so much love gone wrong. That poor Virginia. She'd pull through but then where would she be? He'd always thought she was one of the better women among the Brits.

Open on his desk was a poem by Kipling. The poet had the right words.

> *Oh the years we waste and the tears we waste*
> *And the work of our head and hand*
> *Belong to the woman who did not know...*
> *And did not understand.*

———————

"This new driver will not be so reckless, you have my word for it." Hari Laksman leaned close to whisper in Kamala's ear. "This temporary chap is family's driver. He'll take us to Gemini Circle. We'll hail a taxi from there. That will be best, no reports back to home."

At Gemini Circle, Hari and Kamala got out. He flagged a taxi and stepped into the cab's front seat.

Kamala breathed in the smells of the city. The petrol fumes rising from heated pavement, the underlay of cow dung were a relief after hospital Lysol. Then the city gave way to smoke rising from paddy fields being burned after the harvest. She reflected on Sarla Behn's reading of her astrological chart about a military encounter that could cause mortal danger. Retired Colonel Ian Fitzgerald, rather than being the threat, had rescued her.

Muma Devi heaved herself to the door of the Apsara Inn in a swirl of orange silk like a theater curtain being pulled aside.

"Hari, you are a fortunate devil tonight. And I hear from gossip this girl is off to see Paris. How I envy her."

Hari questioned Kamala with his eyes. "Are you making a journey?"

"A trip to Bombay for dubbing, and then a short stay in Paris, followed by the United States. I shall be back before you realize it."

"Place Pigalle, the Folies. I have never seen those places that are the sources of my imagination. Perhaps it is better that way." Muma sighed. "You will bring postcards and perhaps a small bottle of scent? Now children, upstairs to heaven with you."

Sita, the delicate Assamese beauty, followed them to their room to bring whatever they wished to eat or drink.

When Kamala had ordered Hari's beer and her brandy, Sita still seemed to want to linger.

Hours later, the middle of the night, Sita tiptoed in and brought Kamala a hashish pipe. Sita, Kamala suspected from looking at her pupils, was addicted to opium and had probably added a bit to the hashish. So many girls who came from the hills, Assam and Bengal, had that addiction.

Sita came close enough so her fingertips touched Kamala's shoulder. "Is the sweet perfume Mogul Gardens?"

"It is called Tabu, but the gardenia behind your ear is more entrancing than perfume from a bottle." Kamala leaned close to inhale its fragrance. As she did, the girl uncoiled her sarong. Sita's waist was tiny and perfect, her breasts also small, with prominent dark nipples. Her ribs and hip bones seemed transparent under her amber skin.

"He sleeps." Kamala motioned to Hari and kissed Sita, caressing the women's breasts as tongues went from lips to mouths. Hari woke, looked from one woman to the other and gave himself to their teasing touch. Kamala's breath rose in quick gasps, Sita's even faster. Kamala kept her fingertips on Sita's small nipples until the girl rolled to her back and moaned with pleasure. She placed her fingers where they tantalized even more and didn't stop until Sita cried out. Hari still watched, but after Sita slipped away, he reached for Kamala again, more than ready to match her excitement.

———————

Hari left a wad of rupee notes on the table. She didn't request but never refused money and tucked the bills into her bag before Muma Devi arrived with steaming coffee, mango slices, and buttered toast. They reclined on pillows and gossiped about the night's visitors. "That Sita is a little Nagini, a river snake creature, but she is not prudent," said Muma.

"Does she have a habit?" asked Kamala.

"Yes, expensive enough to borrow in advance. I warn her, but you cannot protect a woman from herself. I have seen too many unable to resist opium."

"I dreamed a dark dream about her. I'll talk to the girl," said Kamala.

"You, my dear, were always of a strong nature, like a silk thread many times woven and rewoven to hold great weight."

Sita entered shyly, her head down. Muma raised a thin eyebrow and left. Kamala slipped off her silver butterfly ring with topaz and ruby and placed it on Sita's slim finger. She kissed the fingers, then the palm, then the wrist. "Sita, you must take care of yourself. Never go to meet anyone outside the Apsara, no matter what they promise you. And think about giving up smoking the dreaming drug. I know its dangers. Most important, dear, do not return to your valley."

"But my son is there. I left when he was just a baby. He's named Krishna."

"Go to bring him here, Sita. I will give you money. I had a dream of disaster."

"Kamala Kumari, I will be ashamed before my son."

"Go to get your son, Sita. Otherwise you will face worse than shame. When I've returned from travels, I will see to other employment for you, but only if you do not smoke any longer."

22.

"You're one hell of a crazy chap!" Fitzgerald pronounced as Jules was getting ready to leave Lady Wellington with Suddaraj in the car. "If this doesn't teach you to stay clear of people and places where you don't belong, I give up, Van Steen. I've patched you up and you'll heal in time. Think now of taking a sea voyage because ruffians who are willing to do this to a man your age might be planning on finishing the job next time. The sea air and quiet will do you good."

Dr. Fitzgerald had admitted him to Lady Wellington after midnight, stopped the bleeding, cleaned up his wounds and kept Jules on pain medication. Jules slept until the doctor woke him by prodding his body for broken bones, examined his wounds and prescribed bed rest for three more days at home and gave him a bottle of pain killers.

If Jules had wanted sympathy, the look in the doctor's bloodshot eyes refused it for his injured body or for his feelings.

"If you know who did this, I still think you should contact police."

"I won't get any help there. It's over and I'll be better soon."

"Do whatever it takes to say out of trouble, Van Steen. This is no game."

"I want you to know, Ian, that the trouble didn't come from being with a woman as you might think. Simpler if it had been." Jules jiggled a canine front tooth with his tongue. "My wife has left me. I know you met her recently."

The doctor raised his fleshy, freckled hand. "Not surprised. She's

165

a pretty little thing but then Americans don't know what's good for them any better than you do."

"I won't argue with you about anything. Tell me, the tire manager's wife, how is she?"

"She's going to live. Her husband is an absolute cad, in a class by himself. Running off with some sort of Malay woman, I understand."

"Her name is Gita and she's been my secretary, a trusted excellent employee. With her gone, I'm closing my Mount Road office. I've got a good man to run the Georgetown branch while I'm away. A Mohammedan, educated and honest. At some point, we'll become partners. I've been planning an extended trip for months and now, as you say, is the time to go."

"Damn right. Keep very still or you'll pop stitches. God bless." Fitzgerald turned away.

Jules had no intention of telling Dr. Fitzgerald or the police what had happened when he'd answered the phone that had rung late two nights earlier. He'd thought of letting it ring but perhaps Rao was at last getting back in touch. Or Angela, needing his help. Of course he would go to her immediately.

A male muffled voice told him that a ship's cargo with his merchandise was being searched. "Come immediately, Sir. Material being confiscated."

Jules had no shipments scheduled to arrive in the next few days. "I'll look in the morning. Tomorrow is time enough."

The command was repeated. "Sir, come now to the dock within the hour. Ship will depart at midnight. Matter of urgency."

Jules hung up the phone. He'd been alone for over a week, hardly leaving his third floor study, Rao's voice urging him on.

The phone rang again. "We shall come to you then."

His heart pounded. "No, don't come here. I'll be there in a taxi."

Jules had known trouble might lie ahead with the boys from Jaffna but counted on guards, stevedores, port police along the docks, allowing him space to explain the point that Rama tried to impress on his sons: violence was not going to win the Tamils freedom in Ceylon. There would only be bloodshed. If they declared themselves part of a non-violent struggle for legitimate rights, he would support them, but he would not continue to do so otherwise.

No watchmen seemed on patrol at the part of the docks where he'd been directed to find his caller. On and off lighting showed only hulls of freighters that had seen better days, bilge pouring out into the oily swells beneath rusted keels.

"Sahib, it is too dark here. You should not step out," the cab driver said.

"If you wait a minute, I'll return or tell you to go," Jules said.

He stood before the side of the rustiest, most sorrowful looking freighter docked at the quay. Were his eyes teasing him? There before him, the *S.S. Rotti* rocked slightly with the current. It couldn't be the same old *Rotti* he'd shipped out on twenty-five years ago from Rotterdam. She'd not been a beauty then, but she'd braved typhoons in the China Sea that had been so bad the crewmen off duty tied themselves to their bunks.

He felt a wave of admiration for the old girl, still above water, carrying whatever they loaded on her like some great water buffalo, head down in the rice paddy. He remembered the Dutch captain, with his white sideburns, Old Chops they'd called him, a drinker who knew Jules was underage when he shipped out but had taken him under his wing. Old Chops must be long dead. The *Rotti* should have gone to ship graveyards long ago.

They caught him from behind, one on either side pinning his arms back, giving him only a second to see there were two of them wearing black masks and red headbands before they forced him face down onto the cold concrete of the quay. After they tied his hands behind him, they dragged him up and across the *Rotti's* gangplank. Coiled rope cushioned his fall on the deck, but he could feel something jab his ribs that was so painful he lost consciousness.

When he came to, they had tied his wrists and seated him in a chair facing a wall so he could not see them.

"You have not kept your word with us, Van Steen."

"Show yourselves so I can speak to you. I know your voice, Arjun, so there's no hiding."

"You are with us or against us." This was from a higher voice. The younger brother.

"Ganesh, I am your father's friend."

He felt a searing pain in his side where someone had aimed a kick. The blow toppled him over, the chair on top.

"Sit him up, turn him around" said the deeper-voiced, older son, Arjun.

"I'm not against you. I assisted you. Why punish me?"

"Traitor." A punch to the side of his head left his ears ringing. Then the ribs again, and the stomach. He doubled over but was caught and kept from falling off the chair.

"Every day the army murders us. They gun us down. We must defend ourselves."

"Listen to me and my old friend, Rama, your father. Your cause is just, but Tamils can't win, even with a few guns. You'll be fighting against an army."

"With us or against us. There is no other way. We will not be so easy on you next time," Arjun said.

They carried him back into the air, cool on his burning skin.

"Remember tonight," he heard Arjun say and then the throb of a car motor.

He'd blacked out on the quay under the shadow of the *Rotti*'s hull. Sirens screeching in the distance brought him around before the Gurka guard shined a flashlight in his eyes

"Why did they do this to you, Sahib?" the guard asked.

"I have no idea," he answered.

"Very foolish, Sahib. Dangerous at night. No place for you. Were you robbed, Sir?"

Jules managed to reach back to his pocket for his wallet. "Yes, I was robbed. I was carrying money. It is all gone."

"How much was it?" the guard asked.

"I don't know."

"Shall I call for an ambulance, Sahib?"

168

"No, I prefer a taxi to take me to Lady Wellington Hospital in Nungumbakken."

───────────

The first call Jules made when Suddaraj brought him home from Lady Wellington was to Rao's ashram in Gandhinagar. In and out of his dreams during the nights in the hospital, he thought mainly of the man who'd put his sanity at risk to assist him, and that he'd found a number but hadn't called yet.

"Please wait, Sir," a man's voice answered. "We will get him, Sir."

After a long wait, Jules heard the phone being picked up and Rao came on.

"I am so sorry to have been out of touch. How are you, my friend? At the moment, I am indisposed to travel but by next week I can come to see you," Jules said.

"I am quite recovered, Mr. Jules. Don't trouble yourself to travel if you yourself are unwell. I have posted one final contribution to our work which you will complete without me. I must return to spinning and meditation."

"You know how much I owe to you, more than I can ever repay, but you'll be receiving at least a token of appreciation from my bank. Shall we see each other again?"

"In the future we will, but for now I wish you health."

"I am sorry I did not come when you were in need."

"No longer any worries about me, Sir. I am returned to peace."

"You are the best man, and will always be my friend."

───────────

In the beginning, Jules believed that Rao had actually found documents and only later began to see figures in his imagination, beautiful girls in and out of his mind like a shadow show with a flickering lamp that made their supple bodies move in a life-like dance. As time had passed, however, it seemed Rao's reports became more imagination than fact, and perhaps they always had been The man's last gift now lay before Jules, certainly not history gleaned from documents but rather a vision seen with burning intensity. Was this perhaps as much truth as could be found in libraries?

The girls had been walking many days to reach the RajaRaja temple in Tanjore. New and beautiful girls joined the procession, coming from Karnatica, the Malabar coast, and Telegu lands, welcomed by the priests promising to make them brides of Krishna, true Radhas for the Blue God, never to be separated from their divine husband for the rest of their lives.

Sunrise turned the sky blood-red. Musicians played their drums and priests carried idols to bathe them. Beautiful Ponni undid her hair that reached her knees. She pressed her palm against the wall, leaving her impression on the walls of the temple, her prison.

23.

Jules inched away from a line of ants dining on pools of sticky orange pollen in the garden of the Das Prakash. The hot sun and bright colors assaulted him, but he felt too weak to move any farther away from the insects, as if their secretions had him held motionless. His body ached with bruises and his mind was playing tricks. The flowering Bird of Paradise bush looming over his table looked vicious enough to bite. Until he closed and opened his eyes a few times, hostile spots in the shrubbery finally turned out to be a pair of white goats munching on leaves.

Angela walked across the garden wearing a soft yellow silk sari with a bright pink *choli* blouse and scarlet roses holding her hair with an artificial black braid for the dance performance. The silk flowed as she walked, as if she'd always worn the sari, reminding Jules how she had floated in the yellow dress when he'd first seen her dancing. His heart rose and fell in his chest with the regret of an older man for a young girl he had to give up.

"My god, Jules, what happened to you?" Angela knelt beside him. "Suddaraj told me you had an accident, but I didn't realize it was this bad."

"A fall down my stairs for tea, working late, not paying attention."

"Are you sure you want to go to this wedding? You don't have to."

"I will go because you will be on the stage. I saw you in New York. I will see you in India."

"I appreciate that, but you weren't in this shape in New York."

"I appreciate your tender voice. You could be angry," he said.

"I'm not, not at all. But you, no broken bones?"

"No broken bones, I assure you. I knew your debut was going to be a small gathering arranged by Francis Standard but that was when I was in the hospital, so now it's the wedding and I want to be there. How did the performance go for Standard?"

"Very well. He seemed impressed that I learned in so short a time and Kamala couldn't stop praising me."

"You deserve to be proud of yourself. I think you've always been too modest."

"I'm learning to take care of myself. Tonight there will be a big audience at the wedding and they know their dance. I met the bride once. She's marrying into a film star family."

"Raj Tewari is the uncle. What will you perform?"

"The same *tillana* I danced for Standard because it's pure dance and I don't have to pretend I understand the words of the *padams*."

"*Tillana, padams,* you've learned all this in half a year. You've surprised me, though what I remember from that night in New York, when I first saw you on stage in your yellow dress, was your bravery. Not bravado but courage in your body. Maybe you didn't know it yourself."

"I certainly didn't show much bravery at first here," she said.

"You were ill."

"That's true. Every day I feel more ready to move on, but I'll miss India, I'll miss Celeste most, and I'll miss my teacher. I am jealous that Celeste gets to go to Paris with Kamala"

"Paris? I didn't know they would be in Paris. I thought there was a concert in New York the Orient Foundation was arranging and a tour to American cities."

"She received an invitation from an Asian museum in Paris, so that's why she's taking Celeste who speaks French. And I think Kamala is dependent on her. Do you care, Jules?"

"What I want is peace and quiet, something I've got to find on my own," he said.

"You asked if you could help me. I've been thinking of enrolling in an arts program, not for performing so much as learning more dance styles from around the world and maybe one day teaching. California will be the best because there's lots of connection with other cultures. I'll like to be near my mother and sister."

"That is a fine plan, Angela. You'll have my support. I'm selling my house and taking time away from business here. There will be plenty of money."

"Thank you." Angela took his hands, then stroked one bruised cheek gently.

"You are going to need a real rest. You'll take time to heal," she said.

Suddenly Jules felt so tired he was dizzy and almost slipped off the bench.

"I'm worried about you, but if we are going, we'll have to leave now."

Suddaraj ran around to open the Memsahib's side of the car door to let her in, then back to the other side to help Jules. *Good, good, they are together*, the young man said to himself. But that wasn't the only reason: every time he saw Baba, he was happy, and the longer the Memsahib stayed close, there would be Celeste.

An attendant placed two chairs for Angela and Jules in the shade of a banyan tree from where they watched Raj Tewari's nephew and Pattu's daughter, so smothered in flowers that they appeared to be idols on wheels rather than humans, circle a fire. Behind the bridal pair stood two priests and behind them, a Gemini film backdrop of Himalayan peaks glowed white and gave an illusory effect of coolness.

"By circling the fire seven times," Jules whispered, "she's promising to be obedient and devoted to her husband."

"You can't see her with all those flowers, but she's very pretty. I met her when Kamala brought me to Pattu's house for a pre-wedding ceremony."

"Ladies and Gentlemen," a man's high voice boomed over the loudspeaker, "I shall recite the closing prayers in English, followed by the Sanskrit."

A crescendo rose from drums and horns.

"Wherewith Agni grasped the right hand of this earth, therefore

I grasp Thy hand. *Dyaur aham, pritivitvam* I am Heaven, Thou art Earth. May they live for a hundred autumns. May they be seeing the sun for a long time."

At that moment, Kamala Kumari, dressed in a peacock blue sari that shimmered around her hips, caught sight of Jules and grabbed Celeste's hand.

"Oh my heavens, oh dear lord, what has happened to your face?" Kamala asked.

"Sahib!" Celeste gasped.

"I was in an accident. Nothing to worry about. Looks worse than it is."

"Who has beaten you?" Kamala kneeled at his side. "Celeste, bring a chair I might faint. You know how I fear injury."

"You sit here, Kamala." Angela stood up, but Kamala clung to Jules' hands.

"Who has done this to you? It was no accident. I know that." Kamala was trembling.

"I don't want attention drawn to myself. Please, don't worry."

The director Prabhan and his cameraman, Murthy, came to greet Kamala.

"That is very bad makeup, Mr. Jules. Someone is doing horror movie?" Prabhan stood back and squinted as if he were lining up a shot.

"Do not make foolish comments, Director," Kamala said.

"That's it, I'll have a new career." Jules still didn't dare laugh for the sake of his ribs.

Prabhan turned to Kamala. "You will be dubbing soon in Bombay? Be certain to speak well of your director when you are in Hollywood."

"You are going to Hollywood with Kamala Kumari?" Murthy asked Celeste.

"No, only so far as to Bombay and then Paris," she answered.

"That is far indeed, Miss Celeste. We will be missing you," said Murthy.

"Mr. Murthy has taken a liking to your girl, Kamala Kumari. He is missing her. He is suffering." Prabhan placed a fluttering hand over his heart.

Pattu hurried to them to add her sympathies. "Jules? What happened?"

"Don't worry about me. I'll have to take better care in the dark."

"Mr. Jules, you've had a run-in with an obstacle. Mrs. Jules, still lovelier than I have heard you were." Raj Tewari raised Angela's fingers and kissed the tips with his waxy mustache. Angela had seen his face on billboards but hadn't guessed he'd be such a short stout man with eyes outlined in kohl.

"How are you, Sri Tewari? This man is adored by women," Jules said to Angela

"You praise too much. I'm squeezed into this suit beyond endurance." Raj Tewari pulled out a perfumed hanky and wiped his brow, removing pinkish makeup. "Indian weddings go on such a long time. Even we Hindus don't know when it is over."

"I hope the couple will be happy," Angela said.

"Two spoiled children. Between us, they have much to learn," Tewari answered.

"Raj, darling." An elegant Indian woman, no longer young but stunning in a heavily embroidered gold sari, placed a long red nail on Tewari's tuxedo lapels. "You have to decide on the lighting. It's imperative you come."

Tewari bowed and mouthed *Shela* as they all followed the woman's swaying hips.

"Shela? Really! How she's aged! We were in a film together not long ago," Kamala said.

"Sahib, may I fetch you something cool to drink?" Celeste asked.

"Thank you, Celeste." Jules fanned himself with his handkerchief.

Celeste walked toward a festooned tent where platters of glistening tandoori chicken, roasted eggplants and pots of bright yellow dahl covered the tables. She poured a glass of lemonade and spooned *raita* for Mr. Jules onto a banana leaf. She picked up one milk sweet and a *gulab jamun* and crammed them in her mouth.

On a nearby stage set, Raj Tewari was directing traffic, yelling at boys installing lights in the trees. Kamala and Pattu walked across the stage as an orange sunset separated into light bands of pink, scarlet and magenta. Kamala knelt to tie bells on Pattu's ankles before she fastened them on her own.

"Kamala, dear, I mustn't wear bells. I've been forbidden to dance," Pattu said.

Kamala greeted her cousins Sima and Bamu, relieved they were on time and sober enough to accompany her. "You won't dance, only help me keeping time," she told Pattu.

"I must not do more. My husband will be watching."

Angela heard the music, drank her lemonade, and left Jules with Celeste to find the stage.

"How is the sound, Tewarji? Echo?" Kamala called out.

"It's good, darlings," Tewari answered.

"Angela, you must join us," Kamala said into the microphone. "Come to the stage."

People were filling the rows of benches, fragrances of skin and flowers in the women's hair rising in the dusk. The drone of harmonium and vibrations of the drum and notes from the flute seemed to set in motion even the branches of giant mango trees overhead.

Kamala kept time with her feet, hands on hips, head sliding from side to side. Servants crept to the foot of the stage. Only the quiet thrum of the harmonium accompanied the dancers as they walked forward to lay marigolds at the feet of a bronze Siva and a blue-painted Krishna set on the front of the stage. A quiet fell.

Kamala listened to Pattu singing the first line of "*Krishna ne begane baro.*" Angela knew the words were about a girl lost in the woods, afraid of the dark, wooed by Lord Krishna who makes love to her. The words themselves weren't so complex but when Kamala sang and danced the *padam*, her interpretation of the phrases and stanzas, could go on indefinitely, always finding new signs of love, new gestures spelling out longing, new notes to praise the god. Her interpretation of the lines were never the same, sometimes they seemed all about physical union with Krishna, other times, the expressions on her face and tonal variations were a spiritual communion.

"Krishna, Krishna, come soon, soothe my pain," Kamala and Pattu sang in unison. They took on the roles of Krishna and the girl playing hide and seek with their eyes and hands, making imaginary parrots on imaginary trees appear at their fingertips, the moon passing overhead, the moon disappearing behind clouds.

Pattu's diamond earrings and jewels at her throat sent prisms of color into the sun's last light as her voice seemed to keep darkness from falling.

"Show me your face, Krishna, so I will not waver in my soul." The refrain went faster and with more urgency. Eyes, hands, voices pleaded, "Krishna, come soon. Where is he? *Krishna ne begane baro.* The sun will not rise without you beside me."

How beautiful, thought Angela who was keeping time with her feet.

Faster and faster, Kamala alternated the roles of the girl and the god, the lover and the beloved as Pattu's smooth voice joined Kamala's contralto.

Kamala and Pattu continued casting Krishna's name back and forth across the stage. Blue-skinned Krishna was everything, everywhere, "All that covers the earthen vessel of my body is wide open to my Love. For Him, I have thrown away all the shame of the world."

They joined hands. "We have seen the endless rivers, the mountains, the three worlds within the mouth of this child! He is Krishna, Lord of the Universe. Oh Krishna, *Sri Krishna.*"

After the *padams*, Angela was to dance the *tillana* beside Kamala. Pattu stepped to the side but stayed near, clapping her hands and tapping her feet, keeping the tala. Angela glanced down at a man who must be Pattu's husband, saw an expression of tension on his round face finally relax as his wife stepped to the side. The air felt so warm and fragrant with all the flowers in the women's hair, that Angela absorbed the atmosphere and forgot herself. She executed the difficult combination of steps and finished a rapid series of foot-slaps that rang her ankle bells beside Kamala Kumari. They both bowed their heads over closed palms. The audience applauded, stood and applauded more. Someone came and placed a garland of intense fragrances, gardenias, roses, jasmine, around her neck. The applause went on and flowers fell on the stage. She saw Jules smiling in the audience.

"You were very beautiful, Mrs. Jules. You danced as if you learned from childhood. You have a future here, perhaps in the cinema we will find a role for the foreigner who falls in love with the older wise man." Raj Tewari smiled.

"That's kind. I'm only a beginner."

Dr. Standard, his glasses fogged, came toward her. "Extraordinary. My congratulations."

"Thank you. They're too kind because I'm a beginner but I do feel an affinity."

"You have understanding and feeling for the art. I can't commit us right now but I think the Orient Foundation might be a place for you. Do get in touch when Ms Kumari is on tour. Jules, of course you're here. I congratulate your wife."

"The praise goes entirely to her. She worked very hard and she is lovely, isn't she?"

"Lovely. And as to the chapters I've now read of your work, I propose to publish a monograph for our programs with Kamala Kumari in America."

"I am far from completing my work," Jules said.

"The material I have will work very well, if you will add a genealogy of the known dancers of the caste. Perhaps you would do that with Miss Kumari?"

"That decision is entirely Miss Kumari's," Jules answered.

24.

In the courtyard, a brindle cow stood tethered to a banyan tree that seemed bathed in gold. Suddaraj's two youngest daughters fed dry grasses, milked the cows and brought half the milk to Meena every evening before the Marwari landlords could claim all of it. Now the girls swept the yellow-red earth until it was pristine enough for Meena and the oldest daughter, Lali, to make a brightly colored chalk *mandala* before their doorstep. Meena then returned to her kerosene burner where she was boiling milk for sweets to serve Kamala Kumari Devi and her companion when they visited.

The way Baba looked as she stepped out of the car took away Suddaraj's breath. She wore a pink tunic and loose Indian trousers, had painted her lips the color of her tunic and her mouth glistened. He'd never seen her in anything but frocks. Her hair had been cut quite short and clung to her head. He lowered his eyes so his heart would stop pounding so hard. Only the youngest child, Baby Ranga, seemed unimpressed. He stood facing the guests on fat legs, the good luck silver coin hanging above his penis. Meena, eight months pregnant, went to fetch a plate of sweets.

"Please eat many so you will return to us soon." Meena pressed *rasgullah* and *jelabi* to the guests.

"Celeste adores sweets. She doesn't worry about her figure as I do." Kamala took one dripping *jelabi* and watched as Celeste accepted two of each kind.

The younger daughters tore into the presents Kamala brought for them, lengths of cloth and silk blouses, petticoats and plastic sandals. For Lali, Celeste had a gift certificate to Higginbothams because Suddaraj said she loved to read. There were bright cotton sari lengths and silk for blouses for mother and older daughter as well.

When the girls had run off with their gifts, Celeste presented Suddaraj with a battery-run radio. "Look here, you press this button." She turned the knobs and music came out at high volume. "Here you adjust volume, and you can find programs, All-India channels play music day and night. You will have company when you are working at Sahib's." They stood close enough to feel each other's warmth but did not touch.

"I will keep all in order until Sahib's house is sold. Perhaps the people who come there will keep me on," Suddaraj said.

"I hope so. I am keeping my room at the YWCA, and there's a chance for a job at Higginbothams Books that would be almost as nice as working in a sweet shop," she said.

Neither of them looked in the other's eyes or spoke until Suddaraj asked,

"Then shall I see you again? I must believe that I will see you again."

"Yes, I promise you. We are friends." She would have held out her hand to squeeze his but Meena re-emerged from their hut carrying Ranga on her hip.

"Thank you. You are good to us, Baba."

———

After their guests left, Suddaraj took Lali on a bus ride to the beach. They rode to the Marina and arrived before sunset. The sky spread a pale pink screen flecked with red and daubed with plump darker clouds, like a baby's muddy feet, Lali said. On the beach they bought green mangoes and had the vendor sprinkle red chili pepper and lime. They walked where they could watch the small waves break on the sand. Suddaraj removed the cloth from his shoulder and spread it on the sand to sit.

"What do you want most, Lali? Do you wish a husband and babies?

Or do you hope to study further and perhaps become a teacher yourself?"

"Papi, I wish to study and teach others."

"You shall have that opportunity, daughter, so you can become like Baba and read many books."

"I will bring all those books home and teach the girls and you reading," she said.

"Will I be able to learn reading and writing at my age?"

"Of course you will. And it will make you happy as it does me, Papi."

"I will be able to write Baba a letter?"

"Yes, you will write that sweet girl. But isn't she returning to Madras soon?"

"She says so but she is going abroad! Imagine. The world should be open for Baba. All should admire her as I do."

They remained side by side until darkness fell, hardly needing to speak above the slap of surf. For the first time in weeks, Suddaraj felt at peace.

———————

Celeste visited Salomé who barely got up from the sofa in front of the new television. Her face was puffy and her body slow-moving. "I am waiting for Kapoor to come but he makes excuses these days to stay at his home," she said.

"Do you think of the *Soeurs* as this time approaches? They would love to see your baby. Perhaps we will go there for baptism."

"Don't be silly. We will have baptism at Saint Thomas, and you will be godmother. It that too much to ask?" Salomé passed the box of chocolates she had been eating from. "I know I must get up and oil my hair. No wonder Kapoor doesn't come." She began to cry. Celeste held her friend in her arms for a long while.

———————

At Higginbothams, she almost missed Rangan who was locking the doors to close up. "How delightful to see you, come in Miss Celeste, you are always welcome."

"I was afraid I would be too late to say goodbye. As I told you, I am leaving tomorrow for Paris. Now that departure is so close, I can hardly believe."

"You must be very excited. Imagine, going all that way Will you be speaking French? Will it sound differently from what you spoke in Pondicherry? Every returned person says that the English spoken in England is different from how it sounds here, sometimes they cannot understand or be understood."

"I am a little worried as well. Not about speaking French but being at that distance. I have been looking at maps. I don't want to sound ungrateful, Rangan. I am very excited about seeing places I have read about all my life, but then I don't know what to expect when I return," she said.

"I spoke to the manager. He was positive there would be a job for you here. You are speaking French so when visitors come, you will be an attraction. Manager likes to say there is no book we cannot find. For how long are you going on this splendid trip? And will you send me cards, please, of Shakespeare & Company, of which I have heard so much. You will walk upon the same carpet as Mr. James Joyce and Mr. Samuel Beckett to whom I will introduce you when you return from Paris. I shall miss you."

"Thank you, Rangan. You will see me soon again. I shall miss you also."

———

Kamala Kumari and Celeste boarded the Air India Caravelle to Bombay. Before takeoff, the copilot asked Kamala for an autograph, and the stewardesses stopped at her seat for her signature. How did you get your first part? They asked. Are you in love with Raj Tewari? Kamala laughed and said that Tewari was a dear friend. "They make him look younger than he is," she said.

Once the engines warmed and the plane began to taxi, Kamala rubbed Celeste's cold hands and wrists with cologne. "A few hours instead of days on a train."

"Train would be fine." Celeste could hardly breathe from the pressure as the Caravelle gathered itself, rushed forward, and lifted off the ground. Below, she saw red earth, the gleaming cross on St. Thomas' Mount and the rippled expanse of Indian Ocean on which ships looked like toys.

The stewardess came. Kamala ordered Lemon Squash into which she poured gin from a flask. Celeste wanted only water.

"In Paris, they serve children wine to drink with their supper. Men order champagne and drink from ladies' slippers."

"They did that in novels," Celeste answered.

"Women of Paris always do naughty things. They live under the sign of Kama."

"In English, they call him Cupid."

"Finally we have time to resume where we left Pearl and Jan. You have brought the pages you have typed from my words?"

"Yes, I am worried. Must we have Pearl going on that boat? My heart was pounding with fear as I typed it."

"I can promise nothing," Kamala Kumari answered.

———————

In the mirror, Pearl applies charcoal to blacken her face, wraps a turban around her head and a strip of cloth over the blind eye. With another strip, she binds her breasts. Old dance pantaloons and a large kurta hide all signs of her feminine shape. She looks like a village boy who has had an accident, and no one will question.

She dresses Jan in a lungi and kurta and darkens his face.

"You make an attractive boy, Pearl. When will you be my true wife?" His breath against her neck makes her heart beat hard.

"After we marry in Madras as you promised, I will be your real wife."

"But now, my darling, why should we wait? I shall offer a prayer to your eternal husband, Siva, to let you come to me."

She rubs Jan's beard with ash, pulling it until he winces. "Sometimes I wish you were truly old. I fear that when we reach the city you will leave me."

"I will not leave the woman I love."

She holds up the mirror to him. "I hope this is true. Remember, walk forward with a stoop."

He doesn't have to pretend to limp. He needs her arm to stand.

They climb in back of the cart with the straw. Pearl has given the driver of the cart rupees enough to reach the first village they come to so he can buy hay for his two bony mares. She doesn't give him more than that for fear he might continue on without them.

The countryside seems to crouch under the scorching sun. Above them, a layer of thick clouds hides the sun and makes the heat more intense. In the stagnant air, no breeze stirs leaves, no birds sing, no monkeys chatter. The horses quicken their slow pace only when they think a shimmering mirage on the road is water. Then they slow, their heads hanging almost to the road and cough, dry long coughs.

Jan faints from time to time from the heat. Once two young British troops question them at a check point. Pearl says her father is ill with fever. They step back from the cart and tell the driver to hurry away with his ill person. The wooden wheels hit a hole and jar Jan awake, but he sleeps again.

At night the driver waters and feeds his horses with whatever foraged dry grasses the villagers will sell. "No rains, what can we do!" he complains when he needs more money. He leaves his passengers to sleep in the cart while he slips off into the dark.

Another day passes under a sultry sky. Jan's fever returns and he mumbles words, cries out and tosses as he had when Pearl first nursed his wound. She let a few drops of his tincture wet his lips and trickle into his mouth.

The third day, the dark cloud layer seems to draw a curtain over the sky so they do not realize they have arrived at the outskirts of Madras.

"You must get down now," the driver tells them.

Pearl pays the rest of the rupees, lifts the heavier bag and gets down. Jan stumbles alongside, holding onto her. At each checkpoint, guards urge the pair forward. Only when they reach the Chaudhury Gate, a pair of Red Coats warn that Madras is no city for the infirm. Jan never raises his eyes. "My father has family who will keep us, respected Jew merchants on Coral Street," Pearl says.

"Jews! They're the hoarders. We should round them up."

At the sound of drum rolls and trumpets, Pearl and Jan draw back into the crowd to watch as the governor of Madras appears with his retinue. He leads the parade standing up in his stirrups and waving his helmet that reflects the strange sunless light. Jan whispers that even during the worst of times, the governor went on a daily parade and made a display of strength, firing off muskets and pushing everyone out of the way on the Chaudhury Bridge.

"He will have all who don't scatter before him whipped," Jan says

Pearl shrinks back but wants to see where another kind of music is coming from. She watches in shock as dancing girls in bright silk saris with gaudy jewels parade alongside the soldiers doing some kinds of ugly gestures to the crowd. May I never suffer this fate, she prays. I would rather die first.

Blasts from cannons and the clanging of St. Mary's bells startle her. She looks up and sees the black clouds massing overhead.

"Hold me up now. We must hurry to Coral Street," Jan says.

Pearl steps away from a girl whose open sores have flies sucking deep in them. "Ma, Ma," she cries. Children run toward them, pointing to their bellies and their mouths. Pearl covers her face against the odors and sights that surround her. It is worse here than in the village.

Jan pulls her forward through a series of gates where sentries again wave them on. "We come to White Town that is closed off from Black Town."

Pearl looks up at houses where pale-skinned ladies stand on balconies staring up at the black clouds overhead. She passes close enough to almost touch one woman, her skin white as muslin. Quickly, the lady turns away as if Pearl's eyes dirty her.

Everything is moving faster now, the wind picks up, the bells clang, carts and conveyances rush by. Capuchin monks hidden by hooded cloaks pass like executioners. Harness men, provision carts and soldiers make a clatter of metal on stone against a stranger sound Pearl can't identify.

"That is surf crashing the walls of Fort St. George. We must hurry."

On Armenian Street, men are hammering closed their windows, boarding up doors before the monsoon winds which will batter them open. Jan rests against the wall of a shop that has "Goldsmith" written over its door. Bangles by the hundreds glitter in the window. Pearl reads words above shops, "Ladies Fashions" and "Maps and Books." Over a picture of a green forest and mountains, she reads, "Home to dear England."

Jan pushes open a door into Montefiore's Diamond and Gold Merchants. Pearl has never before seen a Hebrew, only heard of them from the soldiers. The man has long reddish curls to his shoulders over a soiled grey gown, and fiery red hair coming from his ears and nostrils.

The Jew orders a servant to bring tea and sweets into his office for Jan. Nothing is offered Pearl though her mouth feels parched and her stomach aches for food. She sits on her haunches in the airless corridor chewing a strand of her hair. Tears roll down her cheeks. Outside, winds howl, penetrating the closed corridors. She hears women's voices and smells onions frying. Then something falls heavily on the floor behind the door. For a moment she is afraid the Jew has killed Jan or that he has fainted. Where would she go in the city, alone, with the rains coming and no protector?

Jan pulls her to her feet and drags her toward the door. "The bastard. He takes half my diamonds, says they're to cover the ransom he paid for his son. At least the boy survived and is home, but he's making me pay for it. We wasted time haggling for the rest. Did they bring you their Hebrew food?"

Pearl shakes her head. "Nothing."

"They'll learn to treat me and mine with respect!" She hears loud voices down the corridor before Jan returns with a bowl of saffron rice and water into which he squeezes drops of laudanum. "We'll both need it, to calm ourselves. Drink it, Pearl."

On the shore, Pearl cowers against the wind as Jan bargains for a massoula in which two fishermen have just returned with their catch of small pinkish fish. The fishermen protest that the strangers must think them fools to go out before monsoon hits, but the gold coins Jan offers tempts them beyond prudence. They are small wiry men blackened by sun. One runs to a cooking stall and purchases mutton ribs and rice. Pearl crouches on the ground and eats hungrily as they make their plans.

The fisherman who owns the massoula says they would go only as far as St. Thomas' Mount before night and pull in at a protected cove. If the storm rages they will turn back in the morning to Madras.

Winds are striking huge grey waves slantwise, raising what seem like teeth biting at the surface of the sea and air. Ships beyond the surf toss beneath their flags, the British fleets' red horizontal stripes. "May they sink into hell," Jan swears.

The bells of St. Mary's clang with surges of wind as Jan pulls Pearl into the water and the men reach for her arms to lift her aboard. He holds the purple tincture to her lips and she drinks the bitter draught. Her only thought is that as she drowns, the shell that covers her eye will float away and free her from her curse.

Celeste looked up, feeling dizzy from the up and down of the plane which seemed like the waves that would be engulfing poor Pearl on water.

"We will need divine intervention to help these two reach Pondicherry. I will let the girl call on Krishna, the savior of souls," Kamala said.

"Where will Krishna come from?" Celeste asked.

"He is everywhere, waiting only for us to call him."

"That is indeed a miracle," she answered.

"Why is it so strange that a miracle of rescue happens when we read every year that entire trains are swallowed up by tidal waves during monsoon, while the fortunate people who missed their train or chose a later one, continue in their lives? It will be good for the audience to see the gods flying to the rescue."

Suddenly, the plane shuddered, sank in the dense air as if the falling were never going to stop, but then rose again. Outside the skies were blue and cloudless.

"Ladies and Gentlemen, secure seat belts. No worries, only

turbulence," came a voice loudly in Celeste's ears.

At this moment, a man in uniform was making his way seat by seat toward them. Kamala now froze. A military man.

"Hold my hand, Celeste. If we must depart this life, we are together and our karma will be good in the next one." Kamala closed her eyes and chanted "Om."

"No worries, Ladies." The Captain, a Sikh in white uniform with gold shoulder bars, stopped at their row. "We will soon descend from these clouds. Would you be kind to autograph for my daughters?" he asked Kamala.

"Oh, you gave me such a fright. The plane is truly going to land soon?" Kamala looked up and smiled as she signed a notebook.

"I promise, only a bit more rough air. Where are you ladies staying?" he asked.

"We are at the Taj Hotel, at the Gate of India. You must return to fly this plane now. We may speak later, not now," Kamala said.

"I shall hold to promise." He bowed and turned back toward the cockpit.

"A military man. My heart stopped. A man wearing a uniform is in all of Sarla Behn's predictions of danger."

Celeste gripped Kamala's hand as the plane dove through clouds and then came out over the bright expanse of the Arabian Sea.

After they had their feet on earth again, Kamala led them down the concourse to collect their bags. Once through the glass doors, the air felt sticky and heavy against their skin, a relief after the cold dryness of the plane.

A white Ambassador pulled ahead of the taxi line. The Sikh captain got out from the passenger side and bowed. "I am waiting to serve." He opened the back seat for them.

"Sometimes a bad omen becomes good," Kamala said.

For two days, Kamala worked in the Bombay studios dubbing *Pirates of the Coromandel* and *The Serpent's Embrace*, the Bollywood title for *Veiled for Love.* She sought out a director who made films for television and introduced herself because he seemed never to have heard her name.

"I have two minutes." He looked at his watch.

Kamala said quickly she had a script he hoped he might read one day, something dramatic and historical. It was not yet completed but she would be honored if she could send it to him.

"Please mail pitch to secretary; tell her I have given instructions."

"The studio calls it making a pitch, just like Hollywood," Kamala said as she sat beside Celeste on the hotel terrace facing the Gate of India. Bombay dwellers and foreigners filled the tables, having drinks and talking in many languages. All of a sudden a warm wind came up and the sea became choppy.

"We will not send Jan and Pearl to their deaths. There must be a happy ending in Pondicherry, which you will make authentic with your knowledge," Kamala said. "Perhaps they will be carried ashore and nursed by the women who raised you."

The Sikh Captain appeared on the terrace and headed toward their table.

"This man is too persistent. I'll have to go to supper to appease him, otherwise I will be worried about our travel by air to Paris."

Celeste left the terrace as soon as Kamala and the Sikh departed, returned to their room, ran a bath and ordered through the telephone a chocolate fudge sundae that she'd seen a child eating and wished nothing more than to taste. Then she settled down at the desk and took the first sheet of stationery embossed with "The Taj" and began to write. "Chère Abbesse et Chères Soeurs."

25.

A man selling raw oysters offered Kamala the grey slimy flesh in a shell and she tipped it into her mouth, made a face and swallowed as Celeste watched. Several more fishmongers surrounded them, offering drinks of a clear fiery liquor that Kamala drank and whispered, "It burns like fire." She accepted another swallow and bowed to the gentleman.

Celeste could hardly believe that a day after leaving the sticky heat of Bombay, she was walking in the cool air of the flower market at Les Halles in Paris, France, and she was getting used to the way Kamala Kumari drew all men's eyes to her while Celeste surprised them with her grammatically correct French.

After they finished their coffee, she moved Kamala along before more drinking began. Dr. Standard from the Orient Foundation had given her a small sum to be responsible for Kamala's drinking. "The city of champagne is too seductive," he told her and gave her 200 rupees. "You must see she is safely on the plane to New York."

A year earlier, she'd had only bus money in her pocket and wore dusty sandals that the doorman at the Connemara Hotel had looked at scornfully. Now, in a short navy jacket and pleated skirt, wearing shiny Mary Janes with white socks folded over, she was taken for a Paris school girl from somewhere in *la France d'outre-mer*, somewhere in the colonies, which was true, though few knew that the small enclave of Pondicherry on the Indian Ocean was still French.

Outside Notre Dame, fluffy blue clouds seemed to brush the roofs and spires of Paris. Once they entered the cathedral and were looking up at the stained glass window, Kamala pointed out the baby in the Virgin's lap. "He is like Krishna and the lady is Yasoda, Lord Krishna's mother. I am happy they love him here as we do in India."

"The infant is Jesus, Kamala. The Virgin Mary, Jesus' mother, is holding him."

Beneath another window, Kamala shook her head. "A virgin mother is like the English tooth fairy, no?"

"The Virgin Birth is a mystery. I cannot make sense of the Hindu gods that you believe came from the clouds, but they are not the same kind of mystery," Celeste replied.

"I understand all women loving Krishna as a husband but how can you love Jesus—always so thin and in pain? No lovely dimples like my *Bhagavan*. And does Jesus play a flute for women? Or dance with them? Holy men along the Ganges have bony legs and arms like this Christ but I would never want to touch them and they fear women. I prefer Krishna's blue skin and manly muscles. He loves women."

"I cannot answer those questions. You have to believe."

"I hope you marry a good Christian, Celeste. When the time comes that a proper boy presents himself, since you have no family, I shall provide a dowry."

"I do not intend to marry a man who requires a dowry. I shall earn my own money."

"My! Perhaps you should live here in Paris and meet a Frenchie."

"I don't think so but I want to be able to earn on my own. You remember when you first asked my name and I replied Celeste because my friend from Pondicherry thought my given name was too long to say."

"What was that name? I have forgotten. You have been Celeste all this time."

"Celestine Marie is my true name. I didn't mind being called Celeste but now I am in Paris, I decided that I would like to be called by my French name, Celestine Marie."

"Of course I shall do that. You have a beautiful name all your own, Celestine Marie." Kamala placed her arms around Celestine Marie's waist and gave her a kiss on the cheek.

"Merci."

They walked toward the river, and sat down along a grassy slope where swans floated below among willows. Kamala tossed bread to the floating white birds.

"Let me tell you one of my favorite French tales from the writer, Maupassant."

"Perhaps I know the story because I like the author very much also."

"Perhaps you do. It is about miracles. Once there was a girl who had such beautiful golden hair that no one could pass by without expressing admiration. Sadly, she had no jeweled clips to hold her treasure in place. Her husband loved his wife very much and determined to give her a special *Deepavali* gift. He sold his pocket watch to a dealer for a beautiful comb set with pearls. Meanwhile, his wife was having her hair cut to sell it in order to buy a gold chain for his watch. As her hair fell upon the floor, she wept over it, but on *Deepavali* morning…"

"It was Christmas. I know that story, but it is not by the Frenchman Guy de Maupassant. An American named Mr. O. Henry wrote it, but you are right, it seems French. I suppose that writers must know one another."

"So you know what happens? It is a little miracle. While we are speaking of hair, your bob suits you well. One person approved especially. Our Suddaraj could not stop looking."

"Kamala Kumari, there was nothing that passed between us."

"Of course not. He is sweeper caste, after all, and has all those children to feed."

"Suddaraj is more than a sweeper, or a driver. We are not guilty of a single transgression. There is mutual respect."

"You are quite full of your rightness here in Paris. Just listen to a second story that I am sure is by Mr. Maupassant. It concerns a pretty young woman in Paris married to a simple man who wishes only to please her. The couple is happy except that the wife covets jewelry and he indulges her by buying false stones from the bazaar, the kind we use in the films."

Celestine Marie knew the story almost by heart but let Kamala tell it.

"One night the woman goes to the theater wearing her diamond necklace and earrings. She catches a fever and nothing can save her. Her husband is heart-broken at her death at such a young age and sinks into despair, no longer able to work. Finally, to get money, he takes his wife's jewelry to the bazaar to sell for the small amount he has paid. The first jeweler says the diamonds are real and worth more than he can ever earn in several lifetimes. When he does not believe he asks another jeweler and another. They say the same. How is that possible that a poor man can have bought diamonds?"

"It's impossible to think that he was able to."

"Readers are left wondering, as in many stories by Mr. Maupassant."

The bells of Notre Dame rang eleven, reminding them they hadn't eaten and were still tired from the night of flying. As they walked back toward their small hotel in St. Germain, they gazed at trays of custards, mountains of *éclairs*, *tartes* with fruit that glistened like jewels in the window of a *patisserie*. Kamala chose two strawberry tarts and a chocolate *Napoléon*. Celestine Marie ordered the *Napoléon* and a glazed apricot *tarte*.

"We are enjoying ourselves. We can gain a little weight in Paris," Kamala wiped away a bit of strawberry, "because we are walking the entire day."

They took reverential bites as they walked. The leafy trees held flowering chestnuts like porcelain cups filled with tears.

"I saw my astrologer, Sarla Behn, again before we departed. She still reads warning into the conjunction of war and love. The danger will not go away until there is resolution."

"And you believe this!" Celestine Marie shook her head.

"Do I dare not? I was believing the car accident that brought me to Major Fitzgerald was the military danger she foresaw, but I must be vigilant because there might be another."

"There was the captain of our airplane you thought was military."

"That, too, and nothing happened. But like Anna Pavlova, who believed her bad luck had passed, anything might still be waiting for me."

Later that evening at an outdoor café in Montmarte, Kamala kept ordering a new discovery that Celestine Marie couldn't prevent her from drinking: Pernod with cloud swirls when she added water.

Kamala declared they would stay up all night. "Let us buy gardenias and imagine we are Marguerite waiting for her Armand."

Dr. Standard told me that my birth in Pondicherry makes me equal to a French-born person. I can wash dishes in a café or find a place in a hairdressing salon because my passport is French. Of course I will return to India but I wish to see more of this country before I leave."

"I don't think that's a good plan. A girl your age should not be alone in Paris. No, you will return to Madras and wait for me to come back so we can finish Pearl's story. Let us stop at this café and drink champagne from a slipper."

When at last they climbed the stairs to their hotel room, Kamala opened the shutters to greet the dawn air.

"Now we are really like the ladies in the stories of Paris who are awake all the night." A flock of tiny birds flew up to the sky to meet the sunrise. "I do value you, but you must be guided by me and not speak again of being on your own. My plans for you include further education at Madras Ladies Christian College. What do you think?"

"To study in a college has been my dearest wish." Celestine Marie's eyes were closing but not with the vision of the Christian College walls; she was seeing a small room on a quiet street along the *Butte* of Montmarte where alone at a table by the window, a page of paper spread before her, she was writing.

Kamala made her entrance onto a small raised stage at the Musée Guimée before patrons of the Oriental Arts Society. When her ankle bells stopped jingling, a hush came over the room. Celestine Marie followed and sat on the side of the platform to squeeze the harmonium alongside a Frenchman who was playing drums. Kamala began her program with the Cosmic Dance, posing as powerful Siva defeating the demon and the snake. With a subtle shift of her posture, her pose softened and she became the sinuous goddess Parvati emanating seductiveness from her fingers to her toes. While her flashing eyes never left the audience, she executed a difficult *tillana* pattern and ended with a deep bow.

The fine-looking older French gentleman and elegant ladies seated among bronze curvaceous women and warrior kings applauded until Kamala stopped them with a raised hand. She began a *padam*, her favorite love song to Krishna. The performance was to last only an hour, but enthusiastic applause kept calling the dancer back for encores. *"Ravissante!! Formidable! C'est une vraie déesse Indienne!"*

"They're saying you're a true Indian goddess."

"I have always loved the French, true lovers of beauty. Please tell them that."

Celestine Marie thanked the audience as Kamala bowed her head over her hands and stepped from the stage. She walked to a handsome bronze sculpture of Siva, raised one foot and held it crossed above her knee, imitating the dancing pose of Nataraj, Lord of the Dance. She closed her eyes and stood holding the pose as the audience applauded and called for more.

A small Indian man wearing a Nehru cap slipped franc notes to Celestine Marie who put them in her pocket. Others followed, adding donations to Kamala.

"Such courteous gentlemen," Kamala remarked. "What a pity we have no time to become better acquainted with them and go out evenings. You could speak French and they could be treating us to nights in Paris. Alas, we cannot, but I shall buy a hat for each of us."

"A hat won't suit me, Kamala Devi, and it will flatten your coiffure."

"I want a hat and we will find one to suit you."

On the Rue des Augustines, Kamala bought an expensive feathered chapeau. Celestine Marie chose a blue beret with a ribbon down the back.

"Let's walk up the great avenues like ladies of fashion in our new hats," Kamala said.

They slowly crossed the Champs de Mars, over Pont Alexandre III and up the Champs Elysées to where the grand avenues converged beneath the Arc de Triomphe. Cars rushed past them in constant waves. Suddenly, Kamala was clinging to Celestine Marie's arm. Her forehead broke out in perspiration and her hands were wet and cold.

"What is wrong? Do you have fever?" Celestine Marie fanned Kamala's perspiring forehead and felt her wrist. "Your heart is beating very fast."

"We must stop here a moment. I felt this weakness in Bombay. Now I cannot take another step. A force of gravity seems to press down upon me."

They leaned against the stone of the Arc de Triomphe. In front of them burned the transparent flame of the Unknown Soldier, and through it, apparently transfixed by the same fire, stood a tall man with his head down.

Even before he lifted his eyes and met Kamala's gaze, Celestine Marie recognized and silently cursed Jules Van Steen. Why had Sahib arrived halfway around the world at this moment, in this place? Kamala saw him in the next moment and whispered, "You see why I believe Sarla Behn! She predicted love and war in conjunction and is this not a monument for war? You recall how Jules' head was bound with bandages when we saw him at the wedding? He was also threatened by fate."

"He had been in an accident."

"An attack that could have killed him, but he was saved because we have twin destinies. We are meant for each other. Fate ordains this."

Jules stared a moment and then walked around the flame.

"Imagine meeting you here. How are you enjoying Paris, Mademoiselles? *Quel chapeaux charmantes. Celui-ci vous va bien,*" he said to Kamala.

"What does he say, quick, tell me." Kamala pressed Celestine Marie's arm.

"He says it suits you." She clenched her hands as Kamala continued to tremble.

"You are looking well. Quite recovered I see," Kamala said.

"Yes, all healed." He drew the heavy black hair off his forehead to show small scars.

Kamala pulled back her hair and showed him her own from the accident. "Like you."

Celestine Marie squirmed. Jules looked only at Kamala. How

could these two people believe their scars had meaning beyond the good fortune that they weren't crippled?

"Jules, how long have you been waiting for me?" Kamala asked.

"Waiting?" Jules looked at his watch. "It's stopped. I must have forgotten to wind it."

Kamala pressed her fingers to his lips and smiled. "No, it is time that has stopped for us. There are no coincidences. This moment we have stopped time. Weren't we just speaking of magical events that we could not explain?"

"They were in stories. My watch works," Celestine Marie looked at her wrist. "We have little time, Sahib. Kamala goes to the States by the early morning flight tomorrow. There can be no change of itinerary at this late date."

"Were you in Bombay recently?" Kamala asked.

"Yes. Were you there also?" Jules answered.

"Yes, I was dubbing and we were staying at the Taj of India."

"I slept one night at the hotel."

"I knew it. You see, Celestine Marie, I can do nothing against my destiny."

"We must return to pack your suitcase. There's much to do," Celestine Marie said.

"Surely a drink won't change her plans," Jules said.

"Sahib, you know that the Orient Foundation is waiting for her. If she broke the promises and commitments, they will never again offer her this chance."

"I will go to America, don't you worry. I am not so reckless. But I will not go alone, will I?" Kamala took Jules' hand and brought it to her lips.

"Let's go for that drink. My throat is so dry," Jules said.

"And I am feeling the ground move under my feet. You must hold me up."

Kamala and Jules walked ahead, holding hands, swaying apart and then coming back together as if a current kept them connected. Whatever they said, what reckless plans they made, Celestine Marie knew that she was powerless.

When they reached a café with outdoor tables, Celestine Marie drank *chocolat* that she did not want, even with a double serving of whipped cream.

"I received news from Madras. Two days ago, my house was purchased by the director of a mathematical institute. You always told me to sell it," Jules said.

"Yes, I did. Ghosts inhabited there."

"My ghost in the turret was a friendly one. I shall miss the old captain," he said.

"Kamala, would you come with me?" Celestine Marie made a desperate face.

"Are you unwell? You look greenish," Kamala said.

"Is the smoke bothering you?" Jules asked. "French cigarettes are quite strong."

"Please, Kamala, come with me quickly," Celestine Marie gasped.

"I'll be right back." Kamala kissed Jules on the forehead. "Do not move."

In the small toilet behind the bar, Celestine Marie threw up her creamy dessert.

"That is disgusting. What is the matter with you?" Kamala asked.

"I feel unwell. And I'm worried that you will go with Sahib Jules and miss the plane to America."

"Don't be foolish." Kamala fixed a curl under her hat in the mirror. "Paris fashion suits me, don't you think? I am eager to try the American style. If only I were less beautiful, life would be simpler, and perhaps I would have been more clever as you are, Celeste."

"Celestine Marie," she said as distinctly as she could while trying not to feel sick again, which was disgusting and embarrassed her when she needed to have a cool head. Perhaps there was nothing she could do, like being on a ship in a heaving sea that would take her down with it. Fear made her stomach turn over and she threw up one more time.

"Come out when you're better. The smell in here is making me ill," Kamala opened the door to the toilet and closed it behind her.

Celestine Marie stood against the wall shaking, then dried her forehead with a towel. When she stepped into the café and looked at the sidewalk table where they had been sitting, she did not see Kamala nor Jules.

"*Monsieur et Madame sont partis.* They are gone." The waiter pointed to the avenue.

"They left this envelope for you, Mademoiselle. Monsieur requested that you do not return to the hotel room immediately. The lady said that all was well. *Tout va bien. Les amants. Le printemps.*"

He blew a kiss into the air.

"No, it's not all well." Celestine Marie took the envelope and began running up the avenue, pushing people aside. Kamala Kumari and Jules were nowhere to be seen.

She sat on a bench and caught her breath. Folded in the envelope were 1000 francs and a note written on a napkin. "Jules has carried me away. The key to my writing case is under the mattress. Pearl's story is entrusted to you until we meet again."

She tried to keep tears from overwhelming her. She remembered that when she read stolen novels aloud at night, she never believed in the fairytale love-endings and doubted that Kamala and the Sahib had pure enough hearts and minds to live happily ever after.

She sat for a long time without knowing what she would do, recalling her brave words about staying alone in Paris. She had a passport saying she was a French overseas citizen but the city was so vast, where would she stay and what would she do?

At the desk of the hotel, she learned that Jules had paid their bill for the next two nights. "And what name shall we be using for you, Mademoiselle?" the clerk asked.

"Celestine Marie. Would you like to see my passport?"

"No, ça va," he said.

Upstairs, she counted the francs donated by the enthusiastic Frenchmen at Kamala's concert, money she'd intended to turn over. She had a valid passport with her legal name and more than 1,000 francs from the Sahib plus the rest. With that money, she would find a less expensive neighborhood and look for a hotel and perhaps a hairdressing shop to take her on. Then she might travel to Toulouse or Marseille or wherever Thérèse Bellefeuille was living, before she returned to Madras. As for Pearl and Jan, she didn't know if a monkey king or a fair wind would carry them into the Pondicherry harbor, but they were not her story. She had her own before her.

After

Celestine Marie returned to South India after a year in Paris to a job at Higginbothams on the days she was not studying for a B.A. degree at Women's Christian College, next door to the compound where she had worked for the Dutch Sahib. The screen play Celestine Marie had assisted writing with Kamala Kumari became a Gemini Studios film, though never a hit at the box office, despite the heroine's rescue by a French captain eluding the British on the high seas. "Too erudite" one critic wrote.

Jules Van Steen and Kamala Kumari toured America for half a year, after which they married in Paris. Breaking the marriage taboo that had kept *Devadasis* wedded to deities, calmed Kamala Kumari's anger and her restlessness. She acted in several more films, then returned her attention to the classical arts. Whether Kamala's one child, a daughter, will dance, is not known.

Angela Pascoe Van Steen Vishnamurthy earned her degree from Cal State Northridge in Kinesiology and Choreography. She joined the faculty to teach and stage performances known for their multi-cultural flair. Angela married a Hollywood lighting designer of South Indian descent. They have three children and often travel to Tanjore where her husband's family still lives.

Initially, Tanjore Balasaraswati, the great *bharatanatyam* dancer and singer, had not wished her only child, Lakshmi, to dance because of the stigma long attached to her caste. However, as Balasaraswati achieved international fame and won prizes around the world—*Newsweek* called her "the greatest Indian dancer" and Satyajit Ray made the documentary *Bala*—she groomed her daughter to perform the classical repertoire that had been in her family for eight generations. Beautiful, tall and poised, Lakshmi Knight, married to an American musician, traveled and performed until her premature death. Lakshmi's son, Aniruddha, the ninth generation in the family line, made an unusual choice for a male: to dance in the traditionally female *bharatanatyam* style.

Author's note

All characters appearing in *The Last Devadasi* are fictional and do not resemble those living or dead, with the exception of Tanjore Balasaraswati, the greatest South Indian dancer with whom the author studied *bharatanatyam*; and Abel Joshua Higginbotham, a stowaway librarian who arrived in Madras in the 1840s, and soon after opened the book shop Higginbotham & Co, still a landmark on Mount Road after 150 years. Today there are 22 Higginbothams & Co for book lovers across south India.

Acknowledgments

Thank you across the decades to my *bharatanatyam* teachers Shymala and Ramiah and across the greatest divide to Tanjore Balasaraswati for taking me on as a pupil, and to her daughter, Lakshmi, a friend I still mourn. Over the years, I have been fascinated by the connections and contradictions between the sacred and the profane, and how religious practices have developed to serve men's purposes, while the women themselves, often used badly, sometimes reached great heights of spiritual devotion and artistry. I consulted many books about *Devadasis* but this is a novel and opinions or theories about caste are those of characters, not experts. Phrases taken from *padams* came from many sources, including Narayana Menon's "Balasaraswati". In the background, Colette's novels, particularly *Cheri* and *The Vagabond* played in my mind. I wish to thank my PILS writers, Robin Beeman, Marylu Downing, Liza Pruneske and Susan Swartz for patience and help. Christine Walker clarified with her wise reading. Special thanks to Michael Morey, and to Deanna Watt, for reading the manuscript. For proof reading, thank you Chuck Ferrall, Jane Allardt, Michael Hofmann and Michael Morey. And again, appreciation to Kelly Huddleston and David Ross whose intelligence and creativity I'm fortunate to have found at Open Books.